Igniting the Shadows

By Rebecca Jayne Heipel

First Printing: 2018

ISBN: 978-0-9948656-2-5

https://www.facebook.com/thestrugglewithinRJH/
https://twitter.com/TSW_rjh
http://rebeccajayneheipel.wixsite.com/author-blog

Ordering Information:
Please contact the publisher at thestrugglewithin.rjh@gmail.com

I can never thank my Grandma Lavone enough for all of her love and support not only as my grandmother but as my biggest fan. Her continuous poking and prodding has keep the pen in my hand all these years. Not a day goes by where I don't miss you.

Chapter 1

When Lian opened her eyes she found that she was not at home but somewhere outdoors where the air was cold and dark. She was enveloped in a black mist that felt sticky and heavy to the touch, reaching as far as she could see and feel. The mist felt like thick cotton candy that clung greedily to her body. She tried to push it away but it stuck, gathering around her body. The sticky strands were growing thicker with each passing moment. She felt her heart jump and her throat clench tightly as panic began to set in. A scream gurgled from the depths of her being and she fought back the overwhelming sense of fear that threatened to engulf her. She sucked in a breath of air, but felt her throat clogging with the mist that enshrouded her. She pushed at it frantically, ripping it away from her body and throwing it to the side. But watched it grow instead of shrink. She stepped forward, as if she could walk away from it. Her feet trembled beneath, causing her to trip. She was suddenly falling over, her arms pinned by the mist and unable to brace her impact.

She let out a shriek as she hit the ground, more softly than anticipated with the mist quickly evaporating. Rolling over onto her back, she was tried to push away the mist that no longer existed. Opening her eyes, she realized that the imminent danger was gone and pulled herself to a partial sitting position. She pulled her knees to her chest and hugged them tight. Glancing around, her eyes darting from side to side. Suddenly she back-pedalled herself until she slammed into a tree. It shook above, its leaves gently fluttering down around her. She was still gasping for air when she touched her arms and realized that the mist was gone. Her heart began to slow and her breath grew steady and calm. She lowered her head into her knees and took in a long, deep breath.

After a few moments she looked up at her surroundings and found herself in a forest. A very dense forest with very little light trickling down through the foliage. The tree trunks were a mottled orange colour and the leaves were a mixture of red, yellow and green. She felt a vague familiarity with them, but couldn't remember where she had seen trees quite like these ones before. She leaned back against the tree, closed her eyes and inhaled deeply. As she slowly let her breath out she opened her eyes again and looked down at herself. To her surprise she found that she was wearing a dress; a white paisley dress with pale yellow flowers on it. On her feet were black ballerina flats, neither of which she recalled ever owning. But like the trees, they had a vague familiarity to them. She slid her hands up her body to her chest, or lack thereof, and then her face. She was either dressed as a Lolita or was a child. Her hair was much longer than she had ever had it before and was a mixture of blue, red and black.

She got to her feet and shouted. But the foliage absorbed all of the surrounding sound so her voice barely came out as no more than a squeak. There was no noise at all. The forest was eerily silent and void of any life other than her own. She felt tiny and insignificant, and not just because she had physically shrunk.

Ahead of her, she saw a tiny handmade doll, laying on the ground. She picked it up and as she looked it over, she again felt a nagging sense of familiarity. She had seen this doll before. Had played with it before. This entire forest and everything in it was like taking a creepy walk thru deja vu land.

She was unsure of how she had gotten here but determined to figure it out she set forth to find her way out of the forest. One of these, she thought to herself, must lead out of the forest as she perused her overgrown choices. She started down one, the doll hanging from one hand.

Time passed, but she was uncertain of how much. It neither got lighter nor darker in the never ending forest. She had convinced herself that it wouldn't be that long of a walk, but it appeared that she was wrong. The silence nagged her, chirping incessantly in the back of her mind, like a warning bell that wouldn't stop. There was something wrong about the silence, but she didn't know what. She found herself lost in her thoughts, her mind wandering aimlessly. The doll swung softly in the air at her side and it made her happy. The smile that sat on her lips had not been there in such a long time.

The silence was suddenly broken by an unimaginably loud snap from behind. She whipped around to see what had caused it but saw nothing. Another snap caused the bushes to her left to rustle. She called out to it, knowing how foolish it was, but unable to stop herself. She was rewarded with more silence. A branch snapped to her right and she turned to face it. This one was much closer. The air around her grew cold and she could see her breath as she exhaled. Her heart began to jump about frantically in her chest. Every alarm that existed was screaming at her from inside her head.

She clenched her eyes closed tightly, willing herself to not cry, but felt the tears beginning to well up. Before she could open her eyes she felt the sticky breath of something behind her. Their breath was hot and heavy on the back of her neck. She willed her eyes open and she stifled a gasp as a single nail traced along the back of her neck. She tried to speak but could only choke and gurgle. Her body trembled and shook with fear. The hand lifted a section of her hair and inhaled deeply, letting the hair fall in strands as it slid out of their fingers. She could feel the person behind her lean in close, their breath now hot against the left side of her face.

A soft, feminine voice whispered into her ear, "Run," and she immediately took off.

Her arms quickly pumped along her side and her feet flew like Hermes wings. She heard the woman behind her laugh and she risked a glance over her shoulder. She saw a tall woman with hair like hers, wearing a crop top and a long skirt with a slit up the side. In her right hand was a scythe that stood as tall as the trees. She slowed down as she realized that the woman was just standing there. She wasn't even attempting to give chase. The woman abruptly stopped laughing and locked eyes with her. She slowly shook her head from side to side, as if indicating that Lian shouldn't have stopped running. With a flash she was suddenly in front of Lian, her long bony fingers wrapped tightly around Lian's small childlike throat.

The woman cackled. An evil smile danced on her lips as she said, "I'm going to get you."

Lian was tossing and turning in her bed when Bruce's sturdy hand gripped her shoulder and shook her awake. She flailed onto her back, her long black hair grazing his chin slightly, and stared up at him wide eyed. Her skin was paler than normal and her petite frame looked thin beneath her bedsheet, the blanket having fallen to the ground in the middle of the night. His lopsided smile grinned back at her like an annoying beacon. His perfect hair was honey blonde, chin length and wavy. His face was clear of acne and his lips the plumpness all women dream of.

"Well, isn't this a first? I'm ready before you are." Bruce said with a laugh.

Lian groaned and rolled over onto her side. Bruce pulled her back to face him, his forehead crinkling as his eyebrows furrowed. He eyed her over carefully, placing a hand on her forehead. As he touched her cheeks, he sighed at how cold and clammy she felt.

"What time is it?" Lian mumbled, pulling the blankets up to her chin.

"Nine am. Get up, we need to leave soon." Bruce said squishing her mouth into a fish pucker.

Lian pushed his hand off of her face and blinked her eyes. Yawning, she did a full body starfish stretch and sat up. She scratched her head and got out of bed, grabbing her journal as she did. Bruce stood up and walked over towards the bedroom door. Lian pulled the sheets off of her bed and dropped the pile into his arms.

"Haven't you more important things to do first?" Bruce said, questioning her actions.

Lian pointed towards the closet, pen cap clamped between her teeth, as she began to scribble in her journal. Opening it he discovered two large suitcases, one laptop bag and a small backpack. She pointed to the bedroom door and waggled her finger at him. He rolled his eyes with a laugh and left. By the time he had returned from depositing the bedding in the hallway laundry chute, Lian was already in the shower and her journal sitting on her nightstand. He loaded himself up, backpack slung over one shoulder, laptop bag in the crook of his arm, the suitcases being dragged behind and left the room.

Seconds later Lian popped out of the bathroom, dressed

only in a towel, her wet hair dripping over the floor precariously. She stood in front of her closet, smiling at the emptiness of it. Its only contents, aside from a bunch of empty hangers, was her outfit for the flight. A pair of tight dark blue skinny jeans, a flowered button up blouse and a hooded pullover with their high school logo of an eagle on it.

Lian let the towel fall to the ground as she reached out for her clothes. Her right hand began to shake slightly and she clutched it to her chest, focusing her breath and willing it to stop. It passed by quickly and she dressed, humming softly to herself. She disappeared briefly back into the bathroom as Bruce came back into the room. He held a mug of green tea in one hand and a cheese croissant smothered in Nutella in the other hand. He placed them down on her desk and picked up her towel. The sound of a hair dryer could be heard from her bathroom. He walked over to the open window past her bed and looked out at the tree that spanned their adjoining properties fondly. How he would miss crawling between their bedroom windows, he thought to himself. Although, now both eighteen, they seldom did that as much as they once had. He closed the window gently and turned to face Lian who was smiling brightly.

She glanced at her watch and then back at Bruce. She flashed a giant grin, her pearly white teeth sparkling. "Still have ten minutes to before our taxi arrives." She grabbed the tea and croissant and inhaled them both. She looked back at her watch, "Eight." She grabbed her journal from the nightstand and her towel from Bruce and dashed off into the hallway, calling after him to hurry up.

He raced after her, leaning over the stair railing. "Forgetting something?" he asked.

She shook her head before noticing the damp towel still in her hand. She tossed it up at him and he leaned over snatching it in the air.

He put it in the chute and made his way down the stairs where Lian was impatiently tapping her feet. "Don't you want to say goodbye?" he asked her softly. "We are about to cross the ocean for an undetermined amount of time."

She shrugged her shoulders and pranced out the front door. "Nope. I don't see the point."

Bruce sighed and went to follow her out. He stopped, holding the door in his hand. He could hear her parents in the kitchen eating their breakfast. He gave one last look and closed the door behind him.

Lian's nose was pressed firmly against the glass of the passenger window. As the taxi pulled up to the international departure gates she flung the door open and stumbled onto the sidewalk. Bruce apologized to the driver as he handed him some cash and got out himself. Lian had already disappeared into the terminal as Bruce and the driver emptied the trunk of the taxi onto the curb. He shrugged his backpack over his shoulder, grabbed all three of their suitcases and made his way into the airport.

As the doors closed behind him, he stared at the vastness of the terminal. While he had been in the airport before several times with his mother to pick up his father from business trips, it was the first time he had ever flown himself. End to end rows of people in long lineups, impatiently waiting for their turn to hand in their luggage at the check in counters. People sat on benches drinking expensive coffee while others hugged, sadness choking their voices as they said their goodbyes. Looking to his left he could see Lian, bouncing from foot to foot, her backpack jiggling with each step, her laptop bag swinging from side to side. Her skin had gotten more colour in it since they left and her long black hair, normally tied up in intricate braids, was loose, swaying back and forth. Her mere 5'3" stature compared to his staggering 6'2" normally made her look like a tiny doll in comparison, but today with her energy she appeared almost equal to him in height. She was biting her lower lip, attempting to maintain a poker face of calmness and serenity, but her constant fidgeting and light hopping from foot to foot kept creeping back as did her enormous grin.

Bruce let go of the suitcases and stood upright, his lean muscles flexing as he did. She noticed the beginning of week-long scruff on his face. He ran a hand thru his hair, pulling it all in neatly until the breeze from the sliding doors caused it to fly off in all directions. He gave her a bored look and feigned a yawn.

Lian swatted his shoulder playfully while grabbing her suitcases. "I know you're just as excited as I am."

"Well, maybe. Just a little," he said. He held his fingers so close together that a piece of paper wouldn't fit between them. She went to bat his hand down but her body began to involuntarily twitch. It started as a small tremor in her right hand, but quickly moved through her right arm and into her left.

Her laptop bag slipped through her fingers but Bruce caught it easily. "Klutz much?" he teasingly mocked her, trying to keep the tone light as he put her laptop bag under his arm.

She stopped twitching almost as quickly as it had started. She tried to slug him in the shoulder, but he easily dodged her punch and grabbed her arm instead. Bruce quickly grabbed Lian's other arm and squeezed the two of them together at the wrist. She gave hi a dirty look as he moved both of her hands into one of his, then shrieked as he began to tickle her side. She kicked at his leg and glanced at her laptop which was now sliding down his side. Still holding her hands he placed the laptop between his knees and resumed tickling her. She squirmed about, trying to fight back, but was unable to pull free from his grasp. Her cheeks grew beet red and tears crept out of the corner of her eyes, streaming down her face as she squealed in mock anger.

A voice crackled over an intercom, announcing that business class for the flight to Engelberg was scheduled to start boarding in twenty minutes. The flight attendant talking asked that all passengers please approach the boarding gates. Bruce and Lian abruptly stopped and looked straight into each others eyes, their matching grins growing wide on their faces.

"That's us!" Lian shrieked. She pulled her hands free from the momentarily distracted Bruce, scooped up her belongings, ran for the check in counter with Bruce doing his best to keep up with her. Their line was short and they quickly handed over their suitcases then made their way thru security.

As Bruce put together the contents of his backpack Lian pulled her boarding pass out of her pocket and waved it in the air above her head like a toddler. "C'mon, Bruce. I want my free drinks!" She called out to him. He laughed, shaking his head slightly as he followed her towards the boarding gate. She continued to giggle as their passes were scanned and then they bounded down the walkway to the plane.

Midway, Lian abruptly stopped to look out the window. Her excess energy quickly dissipated as she pressed her face against the glass and looked from side to side.

Bruce laughed and tousled her hair. "What are you, five?"

She rolled her face away from the glass and gave a little pout. "Just enjoying the view one last time. We won't be back for a long time."

"Who knows, we may never come back here," he said solemnly, then laughed. "Unless we flunk out!"

She put her hands on her hips and gave her best preteen poser stare. He tried to match her seriousness, but failed miserably, cracking up. He was still laughing when she turned on her heels and ran down the corridor. He watched as she disappeared into the airplane before casually strolling down towards the plane himself. By the time he caught up with her, she had changed into her pyjamas, had the complimentary headphones dangling around her neck and was fully wrapped in a blanket. Her backpack was at her feet, her laptop bag on her lap and she was holding two flutes of champagne in her hands.

He put his bag in the compartment above her head. "Don't waste time do we?"

Bruce slid into his seat and buckled himself in. Lian took a sip of her champagne, pondered, and then took a sip of his. Bruce snatched the glass closest to him and playfully rolled his eyes at her.

He made himself comfortable as he buckled in and turned to her, a serious look in his eyes. He held his champagne up in the air between them, "To interning in Switzerland."

She smiled back and held her glass up high, "To being the best paramedics ever."

A planet on the far reaches of the Universe

"This is outrageous, I won't be a part of it." Eld said waving a hand as his eyes clouded over. His lips were taunt pulled into two thin lines, a slight grimace on his face. He stood tall and intimidating at seven feet, behind his partner Auld. Auld was more feminine in appearance with matching shoulder length brown hair and emerald green eyes that glittered angrily at the group. Eld's other hand rested on Auld's shoulder. Auld could feel Eld's fingers tense up as he spoke.

Auld set their hand on Eld's and squeezed it firmly. "Nor will I." They said, shaking their head with shame. Not only at the idea the group was proposing but at the fact that neither of them had taken notice of the secrecy that had grown amongst their own people. The group of them was small enough a species, twelve in total, that it was near impossible to hide anything from each other. The two of them knew more than anyone else the difficulty of hiding thoughts given their intricate telepathic connection between each other. They had obviously gotten too wrapped up with themselves.

The others looked at them, their expressions bleak. Never before had anyone so blatantly dismissed another's idea without any discussion.

"But we've always done everything together." One of them said, their voices wavering. The truth being that none of them had ever done anything on their own without the full support of the whole group. Despite the equality amongst the twelve of them, the rest had always looked up to Eld and Auld for guidance. Even though they were all identical in age and had always lived as one unit their whole lives, the two of them had quite obviously been the smarter, more adept pairing and had inadvertently become the group's leaders.

Eld slowly shook his head still holding Auld's hand. He turned his back to them. Auld followed suit.

"Please. We need to do this together." One of them whined.

"You can do this without us." Eld said firmly, although his voice wavering ever so slightly. The group began to buzz like bees in their minds, their panicked words overlapping each other, feeding on each others fears.

"But —" one of them thought and was quickly cut them off with a firm and loud 'SILENCE' from Auld that echoed throughout everyone's minds. The group quickly fell silently and clung to each other.

"There is nothing more to discuss. Do what you think you must do, but leave us out of it. We shall not speak of this again. Do I make myself clear?" they said, the authority in their voice unmistakable.

The group looked at each other glumly. While they all initially had jumped at Darelbaiden's offer, none of the group actually wanted to commit the act. Individually they had all secretly hoped someone else would do the deed or that Eld or Auld would step up, as they normally did. The group was equally bewildered and scared. The prospect of being denied group unity for the first time terrified them beyond words.

'Do we still do it?'

'Why not? They didn't say we couldn't.'

'But how do we not share with them?'

'They've made their choice.'

'More for us.'

'We should go quickly.'

'Its a long journey to the centre.'

'I'm scared.'

'We've never been separated before like this.'

'We will be fine.'

'Hurry, lets go before they change their minds and forbid us to do this.'

'Yes lets go now.'

'Quickly.'

Anyone watching this group would have thought they were mad. Their eyes darted back and forth, nostrils flaring, their hands waving about like they were talking but no words were uttered aloud.

Eld and Auld stood their ground keeping their backs to the group, ignoring the incessant chatter inside their heads. He squeezed their hand gently and felt their smile in return. Since they all were briefly inhabiting a small planet on the far reaches of the solar system and they were amongst other life forms, they were in their corporeal form as opposed to their more ethereal state of pure energy. They never knew if another species would take offence to what was usually perceived as an enlightened state of existence. It became normal practice for them to always enter and leave a planet in their corporeal stage as both forms were natural for them. Their form of pure energy was, however, the only one that they could exist in when travelling between planets and systems.

The remainder of their group, having decided that they would depart, changed into their natural energy state; a mixture of green and blue light energy. The group shot off quickly through the ceiling. Too frantic to think clearly the group had left without checking for witnesses. Eld and Auld sighed, grateful that it was daytime, so it was less likely that anyone would have noticed their departure. When the last one of them left, they turned as one to face the empty space behind them.

"They never think do they?" Auld said softly, careful to use spoken words instead of thoughts.

Neither of them knew exactly how far apart they'd have to be in order for their thoughts to not be heard. Earlier they both felt as if they were outsiders to the groups thoughts. Both believed they had managed to push their thoughts aside. When Eld had uttered an internal groan, only Auld had heard it. Eld was certain that the thoughts he and Auld had exchanged had not been heard by the remainder of the group. But given the groups heightened anxiety they simply may not heard the exchange at all. This would be the first time in the history of their existence, that they would be more than a solar system apart from one another.

"What are they thinking? Do they really think that there will be no repercussions? What if they get caught?" Auld gasped softly at the thought forming in their mind. "Do you think we can survive on our own?"

Eld looked at them wistfully. "Survive? Technically, yes. We aren't as dependent on each other for survival. It'll be lonely as hell without them, but at least we have each other. But I doubt that you and I could perform our duties alone."

Both sat down on the bed at the far edge of the room. They had no use for it; sleep was not a requirement. But maintained it for appearances sake. While knew they never had to worry about neighbours popping by in the middle of the night to check up on whether or not they were sleeping, the neighbours did frequently pop by during the daytime. They would grow suspicious if their living quarters did not imitate theirs.

Eld stroked the side of Auld's face gently, brushing their long black silky hair out of their eyes. "I do like this form of you best. Green eyes suit you well." Eld said softly.

"We all have green eyes, you silly thing." Auld said with a laugh, their eyes twinkling.

Eld cupped their face with his hands and drew his face closer to hers, their lips almost touching. "True. But yours are the most beautiful."

"Whatever are you doing?" Auld's voice nothing more than a mere whisper catching in their throat with a confusing pounding in their chest. There was nothing inside them physically, and yet they felt this immense presence from within as if it were trying to burst out.

"I've seen others do this. I believe it is a sign of affection." Eld said.

Auld's eyes softened as they gazed into Eld's eyes. Auld could feel their body growing warm. "We don't have feelings like others do. You know that." Auld said quietly and the words rang loudly in their ears. The pounding in their chest skipped a beat and they felt their body grow warm all over.

"I'm not sure thats correct anymore, because I am feeling something." Eld put his lips onto Auld's. They felt warm against his and slightly dry. Auld gasped softly and slightly parted their lips, his body sliding even closer to theirs.

Without a moments thought, he gripped the side of their face firmly and pushed his tongue into their mouth. They eagerly responded back by wrapping their arms around his neck.

The two of them proceeded awkwardly, like inexperienced teenagers revelling in their first love; taking each others clothes off, slowly revealing, the difference between their bodies. Despite the fact that they were androgynous beings, they had recently developed variations, similar to those on the planet they currently occupied. To their surprise they had become explicitly male and female. While his change had been minimal and he had eagerly shown them his new lower body contraption, theirs had been more drastic. Until he had disrobed them both, Auld hadn't been ready to confess to him the depth of their changes. Auld had become a she. They explored each other's bodies, finding delight in new senses never experienced before. They joined together as one physically in a way they knew existed, in the species that they themselves had created, but in a way never explored by their own. Auld cried out in pain and delight as they joined and he gasped at the fulfilment he felt. Auld wept at the happiness they found within each other.

The two of them lay in each others arms, glowing in the blissful after effect of their newly discovered state. Both were groggy yet content. These were feelings and actions they had just experienced for the first time together.

"Can you hear them still?" Auld asked, her voice a muffled whisper as she sighed and cuddled further into his body.

"Hmm." Eld pondered, concentrating, "A little, in the far off distance. Why do you ask?"

"Because I can faintly hear them, but I also hear you, much more loudly though."

"Of course you can hear me, I'm right beside you silly." Eld laughed and pecked her warm forehead.

"But neither of us are speaking aloud."

Eld went to retort, mocking her foolishness, but realized that Auld was correct. The two of them were speaking telepathically to each other yet they were isolated from the group. It was like having two separate channels in their heads. He strained to hear if anyone in the group had noticed what the two of them had done, but the group was still chattering on about being separated from their leaders and the excursion they were embarking on. Surely the others would have acknowledged the conversation the two were having if they had heard it. The group would probably be more shocked at what had just transpired between their leaders than what the group was about to do.

The two of them looked at each other, their eyes wide with wonder and amazement.

"Should we tell them?" Auld asked.

He shook his head. "Not anymore." Eld said grimly.

The brilliant greens, reds and yellows of the northern lights radiated against the startling clearness of the starry night sky. A group of dog sledders slowed down as they approached the viewing cabin, nestled within a cluster of trees in the vast snowy field. The tour guide grinned as his groups' jaws dropped, their faces beaming at the wonders above. His crew stepped off the back of the various dog sleds and tended first to their dogs. The guests, still bundled up tightly, were lost in the night sky above them. They were enveloped in the endless brilliance of colours. A couple of them managed to unwrapped themselves from the blankets. They precariously stood up, reaching their hands towards the sky as if the lights could be plucked out. The rest of the group followed suit and pulled out their cameras frantically snapping away.

All except one girl.

The entire ride up she had been all smiles and chatty with her friends. But as the lights appeared above her, her mood abruptly shifted. She grew quiet and apprehensive. It was like someone had told her something that she didn't quite believe, so she delved deep into her own thoughts. She forgot where she was and what she was doing. As soon as the sled stopped, her gaze flew to the forest that engulfed the cabin. The night sky was filled with wonder yet her eyes didn't look much higher than the horizon.

The tour guide shrugged it off and turned his attention to the rest of the group. The tourists could do as they like provided they weren't disruptive to the others or the dogs. None of her friends had noticed her peculiar behaviour, so perhaps, he thought, it was just in his head. He joined the rest of his crew as they helped their guests out of the dogsleds and then began to prepare snacks and beverages for the group.

The forest glared at her angrily. Its whispers emanating heavily from within. Urgent and frantic, desperation pouring from their hurried words. She strained, trying to comprehend what they were so eager to tell her. But their voices were just out of range. The more she strained to hear, the further away their voices got. Despite the lack of clarity, she knew they wanted her to find them. And quickly. The urgency in their voices frightened her. The voices were a mixture of all ages, some tired and gravely, some young and vibrant. She could feel something was terribly wrong. She wasn't sure what she could do to help them, but if she didn't try something she would never forgive herself.

She glanced over at her friends. They were so fully engrossed with the northern lights, taking pictures and drinking hot chocolate that they hadn't noticed she was still in a dog sled. She slid soundlessly out of the sled, the sound of her feet muffled by the layer of soft powder on top of the hard pack. The snow was compacted from dog sled teams, day after day, bringing tourists to experience the lights.

Powder puffed out from beneath her feet with a soft wisp.

Before she could even take a single step forward, an entire pack of wolves silently loped out of the forest from behind the cabin and trotted over until they stood directly in front of her. She gasped and looked back over her shoulder at her friends. They nor anyone else had noticed the wolves. She looked back at them, wondering if perhaps she was simply imagining the wolves. They had surrounded her and the sled. The dogs, nearby, were unusually quiet, whimpering and mewling softly. She released the breath she had been holding. She knew she should be frightened but the fact that the dogs were acknowledging the wolves presence meant she wasn't imagining them after all.

The wolves parted like the red sea, and a lone wolf, most likely the leader of the pack, walked out from the forest, head held high. His fur was fuller, shinier, and heavier than the rest. He bore a patch of white and silver fur on his throat in the shape of the moon. She held her ground, unsure of what to expect or how to behave, as he made his way towards her. The air about him and his stance made her feel as though he was more human than wolf. His eyes, while obviously those of a wild animal, held strength, knowledge, wisdom, and human recognition in their depths. Something inside was telling her that he was very old and much more than what he appeared.

The lead wolf stopped, caught her gaze, looked her in the eye and bowed before her. The other wolves followed suit, every last one of them bowed, giving her their honour and safety. The lead wolf rose, turned and walked back into the forest. Without a moments hesitation, she slipped away into the dark forest after him.

As she looked around she saw nothing but darkness. The faint light from the group was quickly gone. Not even the moonlight could penetrate the dense and oppressive forest growth. She could hear the footsteps of the wolves that followed behind her. The lead wolf was already far enough ahead, that she could no longer see him. She closed her eyes and slowed her breathing. The forest was eerily silent and the pounding of her heart echoed loudly in her ears. She began to think that perhaps she was crazy after all, as the voices were now gone and she was blindly following a wolf into the depths of an unknown forest. She was about to give up and turn back when suddenly screams filled her mind. She clutched her head tightly and collapsed down to the ground, tears stinging her eyes. She stifled a scream, afraid of endangering her friends, whom she felt were at risk just being this close to her. The voices, wherever or whomever they were, were in danger also.

The screams subsided until there was just a lone whisperer. A soft, quiet, feminine voice. Most likely a young girl barely into adolescence. Getting to her feet, she opened her eyes and began to walk in the direction she could hear the voice coming from. It was calling out to her, urging her to come quickly. She began to jog, then run, as the voice, in return, began to yell out directions. Warning her of trees, undergrowth and other obstacles. She could feel branches whipping along her face and hair, bitting into her skin, leaving small trickles of blood behind. As the voice grew louder and louder it felt like the girl was running along right beside her, whispering directly into her ear. Then the other voices began to chime in, urging her to run even faster.

As she had disappeared into the forest, Bruce had turned to offer her a hot chocolate. He saw the sled empty and the dogs cowering together. Hearing a scuffle Bruce looked towards the forest and saw the tail end of the pack of wolves disappear into the forest behind her. He made his way towards the forest but the wolves were already gone. He shined his flashlight through the trees and saw only shadows dancing and flickering about. He was about to turn back to the group when out of the corner of his eye he thought he saw movement. A flash of pink, the same colour as her jacket. He turned back towards the forest and made his way in, calling out her name as he did.

She could hear the pounding of the wolves paws against the snow in her mind as they kept pace with her. The lead wolf was somewhere ahead of her, clearing the path of danger. Further and further into the forest she ran, the darkness enveloping her body like a second skin. Her heart hammered loudly. She could feel her breath as it bounced off her scarf and into her face.

Abruptly, the forest opened up into a small clearing, approximately twenty feet wide and forty feet deep. It was taken up mostly by a large pond with several large chunks of ice floating in it. The back of the pond disappeared into the forest and the moonlight shone in broken fragments through the branches and leaves. At the edge of the pond was the lead wolf. She walked up to him, knelt down and patted his head. She thanked him for bringing her there, stood up and began to unzip her jacket.

Bruce had barely made it into the forest when several wolves surrounded him. Bruce tried to back away only to end up against a tree that hadn't been there a moment ago. When he tried to step away from the tree the wolves growled at him. Not a threatening growl, but definitely a warning. Bruce looked from wolf to wolf, wondering how he was going to get out of this situation and where she had wandered off too. He was very worried about her. Something about her had been off all week. She had been isolating herself from the group and even himself.

Bruce felt a tug on his pant leg and looked down. One of the wolves had grabbed his pants with its mouth and was pulling it. He tried to shake it off but the other wolves growled at him as the other wolf tugged him forward. Surprised, he reached a hand down to the wolf, patted its head and asked it if it wanted him to follow. The wolf tugged at his pant leg again while the others howled. He pushed himself away from the tree and took a step forward. The wolf let go and trotted off ahead towards the pond.

Bruce broke into the clearing as she dropped her last piece of clothing onto the ground and took a step into the freezing cold pond. He called out to her, frantically running towards her. She got knee deep before Bruce managed to catch up and grabbed her hand. She turned to face him and he gasped loudly, dropping her hand.

Her eyes were glazed over and filled with a milky blue light. She cocked her head from side to side and looked at him with confusion. He stroked her cheek, begging her to come out of the water and join him. She tried to turn back, away from him and into the water, but he grabbed her arm. She stumbled, almost falling over, but he caught her. She looked up him again, the milky blue light turning dark. She pushed herself out of his arms as she stood up. Her eyes filled with tears and spilled freely, turning to ice as they rolled down her warm cheeks. Her dark blue eyes turned back into milky blue and then the strange light disappeared entirely. She shivered and recognition filled her eyes.

"What's happening to me?"

Lian had managed to outrun the she-demon in the forest. Her clothes and hair had changed, but she was still a child. Appearing maybe ten years of age. But she felt, much, much older. Hundreds, if not thousands of years old. She wasn't sure where she was or where her family had gone. She wasn't sure if she was on the same planet as the she-demon or not, nor did she really care. She and her family looked very plain compared to the other people that lived in the village. An advantage that worked for them as they tried not to stand out. Not only were they welcomed with open arms, as they usually were wherever they travelled, but she was doted upon for the youth like appearance she had.

Looking around Lian realized she was now sitting at the centre of a village on a moderate sized water fountain made of a dense grey stone that appeared to be mottled yet was smooth and cool to the touch. She dipped her hand in the water, swirling it around. The water was crystal clear and the sunlight glistened brightly off of it. In the centre was a statue of the woman whom had given birth to the village, or so the legends told. The woman had a gentle face with soft features that looked kindly upon the village.

There were several children playing around her. Girls braiding each others hair, boys chasing their various pets or playing a unique version of hopscotch. A couple of the girls had invited her to join them but she had politely declined. The girls braiding each others hair had looked longingly at her free flowing hair. Being that it was as long as they were tall. She might look like a child on the outside, but she most definitely was not. Her parents were the only people that didn't treat her like an infant. Even the rest of her family talked about her as if she were an invisible child with a plague like disease, avoiding her at most costs. Because of her youthful appearance, she was often left out of the family's discussions with village elders as they travelled. Not that she minded. She had never cared for the politics involved in the 'family business' and she had always known that despite her capabilities, she would never follow in their footsteps. Quite the opposite in fact. But she had to bide her time before changing paths entirely. She still had a lot to learn before she could venture off on her own and she loved her parents fiercely. She wanted to stay with them as long as possible. She was also a little afraid that they wouldn't understand her choices, or lack thereof.

Tired of sitting she decided to explore the village. She had felt there was something special about this village when they first arrived and she was determined to figure out what secrets it held. She walked down the main road for a few minutes before she came upon a small alleyway. She looked around, saw no one and darted down it. It wound about, turning up a set of stairs, down another set of stairs and then became a small tunnel under an overpass of some kind, before finally splitting into two paths. One to the right led back to a main road and the one to the left looked to go into a very dark, unlit, and possible scary tunnel.

So she went to the left.

The tunnel continued to grow narrower with moss like foliage growing on the sides, damp to the touch. It clung to her clothes and threatened to pull her into the walls of the tunnel, like leeches threatening to eat her alive. She smiled silently at the thought. The tunnel came to an abrupt end as she bumped her head, walking into the wall in front of her. She rubbed her forehead gingerly as she knelt down and felt around the edges of the wall. It was soft and springy beneath her touch. After several minutes she pulled most of the moss off of the wall and found a solid surface beneath. There was wood along the outer edges and glass in the centre. She smiled, guessing that she had found a long forgotten window to someone's cellar.

It took quite a bit of effort, but she managed to slide it open just enough to let herself through. The drop to the ground was less than six feet and she landed with a soft thud on a dirt ground, a cloud of dust and debris flying up around her. She stayed hunched down until the dirt settled and her eyes had adjusted to the darkness. She was fairly certain that she was alone. Based on the overwhelming musty smell it hadn't been used in quite some time.

With one hand on the wall she made her way around the cellar, finding empty shelves, potatoes so overgrown they had rooted into the cellar shelving and the odd jar that sloshed about when she shook it. Despite her curiosity, she didn't dare open them. She finally found a set of stairs leading upwards. She cautiously made her way up them, careful to test her weight on each step for both for noise and sturdiness. When she finally made it to the top she opened the door a crack. Thankfully, it swung inwards and directly in front of the door was a large wooden cabinet. The back of the cabinet had enough holes and cracks that she could detect movement and hear voices murmuring in the distance. A quick check behind her confirmed that there was no light escaping from the cellar behind. She could leave the door fully open as she pressed herself up against it.

It was too dark for her to ascertain who the people were, but the voices were familiar enough that she recognized her family. She thought it odd that the officials they were visiting wouldn't have a cellar full of wine and other treats as they usually were the most wealthy in town. Although they seldom ate food, her family would often tell her about the large spreads of food presented before them. It appeared to be a universe wide custom to greet others with an abundance of food and drink. She had always felt it more a way of bragging than anything else. But she had learned to keep such opinions to herself as it often upset her family when she spoke so freely. She could make out from the snippets of conversation that they were in an abandoned shop on the outskirts of town and that they were not with town officials. The were also heatedly discussing someone in particular. Someone they were greatly afraid of. She could hear her parents constantly trying to reassure the others, although this person they feared was strong and very powerful. She thought she heard them debate on whether or not something was 'wrong' with this person. They thought she was a threat to them all and urged her parents to side with them.

As she pressed her ear closer to the cabinet and the conversation continued on, she realized that they were talking about her. They were afraid of her. She put a hand to her mouth as she gasped. She squatted down and waited, but their conversation continued on uninterrupted, so she knew that they hadn't heard her. Tears sprung from the corners of her eyes. She had always done her best to hide her true self from them, to hide her immense powers. Her parents knew, of course, but they had urged her to remain quiet about it from a very young age. They had explained to her many times how the rest of her family was sterile and they were all that would ever exist. How her birth was as much an anomaly as it was a miracle. She knew that she was different but she had always hoped the rest of them would accept her as her parents had. But now she knew it wasn't to be. That her time to leave would be much sooner than she expected.

She rose up, closed the door behind her and made her way down the stairs into the dark depths of the cellar. She let out a sob, trying to choke it back. Not realizing that she had physically aged almost five years since she had first stepped into the cellar.

Chapter 2

Lian's eyes snapped wide open. Her breath was ragged and her skin covered in a sticky cold sweat. Her hands were clenching her legs tightly, fingers white to the knuckles and her fingernails imbedded deep enough to break skin. Her cheeks moist from tears, her teeth clenched making her breath escaped in a slow hiss. She relaxed her hands, letting go of her legs and wiped her face dry. She could feel her hands trembling and she quickly clutched them together, pressing them down into her lap. Trying to steady them before Bruce or anyone else could take notice. She turned to her left to face Bruce, worried that he might have heard her wake up. But she saw him in a similar state of agitation himself.

He turned to face her and his eyes popped open wide with surprise and bewilderment. He stared right thru her as he gulped in his breaths hungrily, gasping for air. His skin was ashen and covered in sweat, she could see his chest pulsing heavily with each breath as his body trembled slightly. She could also see much more than she or anyone else for that matter, would want to beneath his track pants. At least his dream appeared to have been somewhat pleasant. Her lips made an attempt at a half smile as she was trying to contain her own emotions.

He looked over at her, "Bad dream?" he asked softly, not entirely aware yet of his surroundings.

Lian nodded as she leaned down to retrieve her purse from her feet. "You too?" she asked as she rummaged through it until she produced a bottle of prescription medication. She popped the cap open easily and threw two blue pills in her mouth. Bruce handed her a bottle of water and she took it, her hands still shaking slightly. She quickly swallowed the pills and put the water bottle in-between her legs, hoping he hadn't noticed how badly she was shaking. The tremors were getting more and more frequent and her dependency on her medication had increased immensely recently. Much more than she cared to admit, especially to him. She snuck a look at him and saw he was too busy trying to cover himself up with a blanket, then a pillow, then the pillow under the blanket. He caught her looking at him and his face grew bright red. He asked if she was okay and she gave him the biggest grin possible and nodded her head, hiding her pain beneath the amusement of his predicament. He grabbed her water bottle, brushing her leg roughly with his hand. She sighed, relieved that he hadn't noticed anything unusual in her behaviour. She brushed off the idea of the nightmares being anything more than her nerves. She pulled her nightmare journal out of her bag and opened it on her lap.

He handed her the now empty water bottle and she tucked it into the back of the seat in front of her. "Couldn't save the princess?" she asked absently.

Bruce, still flustered, cracked a half smile, "Had only just found her when I woke up."

"Hmmm. That sucks. Was she at least hot?"

Bruce shook his head and gave her a look of surprise, "Really?"

She shrugged her shoulders, "No point in being upset if

she wasn't worth saving."

Bruce stared at her, trying to asses the seriousness in her face. She cocked her head slightly and batted her eyelashes. He looked at her stunned for a moment, then roared with laughter. Tears streamed down his face and he pounded the armrests with his hands. She was still staring at him when his laughter finally started to subside. The two of them realized that the entire business class section was staring at them, judgement and distaste in their eyes.

"A simple yes or no would have sufficed."

Bruce went to give a witty comeback when the intercom came to life and the pilot announced that they were beginning their final descent. Everyone began to buckle their belts and put their trays up. Lian took Bruces hand in hers, squeezed it tightly and smiled.

The centre of the Universe

There were seven of them. One representative each from seven different species. More than that would would trigger the alarms and less could arouse suspicion. Currently there were seven species that were allowed in the inner sanctum of the greater depths of the universe. These species were granted access to all information documented in this specific existence of the universe; everything that had ever happened since the dawn of time. They were given the opportunity to use their intellect to either guide other species with small nudges or to help those lost beyond hope to peacefully move forward. It was a rare privilege, given only to a select few species and only when they was a sufficient number of them. This stopped any one species from taking too much burden on and, in case of regression, also prevented the ability to abuse the power that was bestowed upon them.

It had been several decades since any of the select seven had last visited and hundreds of years since all seven had come together. It was common for them to not re-convene after their initial visit. Often once was plenty for them to realize their ultimate purpose and would seldom return unless they found themselves in a predicament too difficult for them to solve. They found that although the sanctuary of this space was most comforting and pleasing to their minds, it was all too alluring. As well, it was nestled far enough in the inner makings of the galaxies that it was difficult to coordinate all seven of them to convene at once.

The eighth member of the current party was the Gatekeeper. He had approached Darelbaiden, the unofficial leader of this wayward group, a few hundred years ago with the proposition. Although he himself seldom left the inner sanctum of the universe, he had had many opportunities to overhear the enlightened ones chatter about the many species within. Darelbaiden's species in particular, was a favourite topic of theirs as they were consistently unpredictable beings. In one century they would be on the border of self extinction and in the next they would be incredibly prosperous. Darelbaiden, in particular, was a strong and formidable leader. He was extremely ruthless and had single handedly destroyed an entire alien invasion on his planet. He had overheard enough about Darelbaiden to know that this man could help him achieve what he alone could not. Freedom from his current existence.

It had not taken much to convince Darelbaiden of his plan. The promise of eternal life was all the Gatekeeper needed to mention to peak his interested. However, getting him to agree to share the eternal life with six other species had been the most difficult hurdle to overcome. There were several safeguards to enter the room of the inner psyche. Only he, the Gatekeeper, could enter it alone or with any combination of the seven enlightened ones. It was a failsafe to protect the contents and knowledge contained within. The Gatekeeper could enter the room and assist them with accessing the information, but he himself could not access or view the information. In fact, for several millennia only he could enter as there hadn't been enough species to open all of the gates at the same time. The was a minimum requirement of three with a maximum of seven.

Over the next several decades Darelbaiden went about recruiting different comrades of different species. Those weak enough to bend to his will easily yet strong enough to not cower at the last minute. It was essential that they all be from different origins or the failsafes would not be released. They had decided upon seven in case one or more of them bailed at the last minute. He choose the Nomda's, a race of travellers who were essentially homeless and lived, bred, and died on their space ships. There were stories telling of them having never had their own planet and that they were constantly looking for a home while other stories say they were simply restless and inquisitive. They had knowledge of the various other galaxies within the universe and he knew that the prospect of a longer life would make them ideal companions in this adventure as it would allow them to traverse even farther then they already had.

The Eldross were a small sized species, with only twelve members in their entirety. While they didn't require extended life, they were an energy form in their normal state, the power they could obtain would allow them to retain their corporal form longer and more frequently than normal and allow them to visit the planets they worked on more easily.

The Sawians were a race of peacekeepers who constantly complained about their inability to survive the rough terrains and conditions associated with their profession.

The Dragonians were a reptile like race that accidentally

destroyed their own planet and had assembled poorly crafted spaceships that were constantly on the verge of self destruction.

The Napravatian's were a race that created planets and often died after finishing only one planet. The physical energy required to create a planet often wiped out entire families at a time.

And finally he had chosen the Remkins. They were quiet, timid and quite meek. They were also under the rule of his race, the Rangnorokians. They would do as they were told with no questions asked.

Each species selected one representative, the most trusted, or gullible one, and had sent them across the galaxies on this journey. They had all met up in the Anoria Galaxy, a short journey away from the universes core. There, Darelbaiden had taken them aboard his ship and flown them in on a secret path provided to him by the Gatekeeper. One promised to not raise alarms or attention. The Gatekeeper, thankfully, had been true to his word.

They boarded the station and with remote access, the Gatekeeper guided them via the intercom towards the inner sanctum. They walked corridor upon corridor, passing nothing more than windows filled with the vastness of space that surrounded them. Endless corridors that wrapped around each other, looping the weak minded and faint hearted. Only those who were sound of mind would sense the right path to go. Or those guided by the Gatekeeper. When he saw the seven of them on the other side of the main door, he smiled in relief. He rolled the large metallic circular door open and they immediately began to pile in, mesmerized by the glowing ball of brilliant blue light held afloat above a large torch in the centre of the room. The Gatekeeper held his hands up high and stopped them. He raised a finger to his lips, promptly quieting the group. He then held up a single finger and indicated that they should follow him, but only one at a time. The Remkin representative went first. He was led along a narrow pathway, lit by brilliant colours that changed as he walked, to the opposite side of the room and was left standing behind a large organic looking console. It appeared to grow from the floor beneath, much like a tree and bore the fruit of a single computer screen. Quite a mixture of components; life and technology. One by one the Gatekeeper led each person to a single console and left them without uttering so much as a single word.

When they were all deposited at their respective consoles, the Gatekeeper moved towards the centre of the room. The ball of blue light was directly behind him as he took his place beside the console. He placed his palm on a holographic screen that appeared suddenly and pressed down lightly. The other consoles immediately lit up. A laser beam jumped out from the consoles, split open wide and scanned each of them. Then, the outline of a hand relative to the species glowed on the console in front of them. One by one, they placed their hands in outline on the screen. The screens flickered beneath their palms until they finally settled upon a bright white pulse. As each console pulsed white the Gatekeeper looked around the room, his heart clenched tightly inside his chest. When the final console flashed white, his console in turn went green and the others began to pulse red. He quickly punched in a sequence of codes. His console too flashed red and then they all abruptly shut off. The blue ball of light in the centre of the room began to pulse rapidly, like a heartbeat that was growing more and more excited by the second. It pulsed quickly at first, then began to slow down; like time was starting to stop. Before it could come to a complete stop, it abruptly snuffed itself out. The Gatekeeper turned to face the group, his face full of excitement and disbelief. He hadn't actually expected it to work.

"Quickly, while the shield is down, we must hurry." The Gatekeeper said, urging them to come closer.

Darelbaiden, the first to react, looked inside the torch and saw a large blue crystal. It was twelve inches in diameter and three inches thick. He picked it up and was blinded by the reflection it produced. He felt something tug painfully at his soul and he gasped. He held it close to his head and shook it. "What do we do with it?" He asked, "How does this work?"

"You must break it." The Gatekeeper said.

"What are you insane?" the Eldrossian proclaimed loudly.

"Its the only way to be able to leave enough behind for the station to keep running. Break it up and split it amongst us. But hurry, we don't have much time before the shield comes back on. You all need to be back at the consoles before it does." The Gatekeeper said anxiously.

Darelbaiden looked at him skeptically. The Remkin, despite his race's usual meek demeanour, took the crystal out of Darelbaiden's hands and threw it onto the ground. It shattered into several pieces of varying sizes. The group then swooped in like vultures and gathered all of the pieces, stuffing their pockets full. The Gatekeeper was only able to snatch a couple of small slivers for himself. A small ticking noise suddenly came from The Gatekeeper's console and a ten second timer started audibly counting down.

"Hurry! back to your console, put your left hand on them." The Gatekeeper yelled at the group as they dispersed and retook their positions at their appropriate consoles. As the timer was about to hit zero the Gatekeeper realized that there were no crystal fragments inside the torch. Without them, the system would be unable to function properly and their actions would be detected. His breath caught in his throat as he threw the only fragments he had into the torch, hoping it would be enough. The shield came back on as the Gatekeeper put his hand back on his control console. They all stood silently, waiting for the alarms to come on, but nothing happened.

The Gatekeeper turned to the group and gave a meek smile. He switched his left hand for his right hand on the console and their consoles shut off. The Gatekeeper waved towards the group, indicating that they should follow him back to the main door. He let them out of the room, one by one. The group could barely contain their excitement and their nervousness. They still had to get out of the station and the inner sanctum undetected. The last one to exit was Darelbaiden. He reached out and shook the Gatekeepers hand. His grip was firm and the smile on his face was larger than life.

He patted the Gatekeeper's shoulder. "Good job mate," Darelbaiden said.

Darelbaiden squeezed his shoulder before releasing it and quickly taking a step backwards, pulling the door closed between them. Without taking his eyes off the Gatekeeper he locked the door. The Gatekeeper gasped as he realized that he had been tricked and Darelbaiden wasn't going to free him from this prison.

The taxi pulled up outside a large dormitory just as the sun was setting. The red and orange light splashed against the building. It created the illusion of a semi haunted horror house instead of the postcard picturesque building she had imagined from the online brochures. The architecture was much older than anything they had back home. Lian pressed her face against the glass, again like a small child, and stared out the window in wonder. Bruce chuckled as he paid the taxi driver before getting out and grabbing their suitcases out of the trunk. Lian continued to stare through her window. A mischievous grin grew on his face as he leaned over and opened her door, causing her to fall out. He burst out laughing as she scrambled to her feet, wiping the dirt off of her pants and shooting him a look of disdain. He innocently shrugged his shoulders, grabbed their suitcases and headed towards the front of the building. She grabbed her carry on stuff and begrudgingly followed him inside, murmuring obscenities under her breath.

Inside the main entrance was a small and more modern looking receptionist desk. The lights, however, were off and a sign stated their operating hours were '0800-1700'. The clock above showed it was well past operating hours. They looked around for signs of life.

She returned from the hallway, "They knew when we were arriving, did they not?"

He nodded and leaned over the counter. He smiled as he produced an envelope with their names written on it. She snatched it out of his hands and ripped it open, sticking her tongue out at him. He rolled his eyes at her and shook his head. Inside she found several papers, including a map, a welcome letter, and their room keys. According to the map it was best for them to go back outside and walk around to the back. She pointed towards the back door and he followed her, suitcases in hand.

Outside again Lian stopped for a moment, took a deep breath in, and exhaled slowly. "This air tastes so much better than back home. My lungs feel so light."

Bruce inhaled deeply and exhaled slowly a few times. He shrugged his shoulders and walked on. She looked at his back and smiled. It was just like him to not take things as seriously as her, remaining carefree and aloof as always. They slowly walked along the outside of the building, following the cobblestone path. They were both too exhausted from the fifteen hour flight to really take in the beauty of the scenery they were meandering through, but they were happy to be outside and walking. The view of the mountain side was breathtaking, but she could barely keep her eyes open long enough to follow the map.

Consulting her map once more she pointed towards a semi hidden stairway. They looked around for an elevator but found none. Bruce easily carried both their suitcases up the three flights of stairs in one trip. One on his shoulder and the other he held on his side like a sack of potatoes. He was waiting for Lian at the top with a giant grin on his face. Huffing, she ignored his grin and followed him as he led them down a hallway until they reached where it ended with two corner rooms. There was a fire escape on one side of them and a broken elevator on the other. He was still sporting a goofy grin. She looked at him questioningly. He pointed to the rooms and held up the envelope with the keys. She was still confused as he took the keys out of the envelope and dangled them in front of her face, pointing to the room numbers on the doors. Her face lit up like a Christmas tree. She frantically pulled their room keys from his hand, only to drop them on the ground in her excitement. Bruce laughed as he picked them up and opened a door with gusto. "Ta Dah!" He exclaimed. Their rooms faced the mountains where the sun was setting and they shared a bathroom. She wouldn't have to share with a complete stranger.

She walked into a pitch black room and sighed, her enthusiasm briefly curbed. They could have at least left the curtains open she thought. She felt along the wall until she found the light switch and flicked it on. Slowly she took a few steps into her room and then turned a full circle. She couldn't believe what she was seeing, or more what she wasn't seeing. Her whole room was empty. Absolutely bare. A wooden frame built into the wall under the window was the only thing she could see.

"Bruce!" she called out to him as she walked thru their adjoining bathroom into his room. "Bruce! You're not going to —" she stopped mid sentence as her jaw dropped. All of her furniture had been piled inside his room and mixed with his. Their mattresses had been place precariously atop of two armchairs, making a makeshift fort complete with blankets draped over the whole thing. His desk had been flipped upside down with hers set carefully atop, feet upon feet. He was standing shell shocked in the middle of his room, his suitcase askew at his feet.

Suddenly, the lights began to flicker and room filled with laughter as people began to pile in en masse. Lian and Bruce stood in the middle of his room, back to back, as a plethora of students piled into the room and began rapidly introducing themselves. They shook more hands than they could count and promptly forgot each name as a new one was said. In a matter of minutes the welcoming committee disappeared as quickly as they arrived and the furniture was all still inside Bruces room.

"Well, unless you want to share a bed I guess we better move this stuff back to my room," Lian said raising a hand towards the pile and discovered that she had a beer in her hand. Bruce looked at his hands and found two, a beer in each of his hands. They smiled and took sips of their respective beers. She set hers down on one of the desks in his room and smiled. "Lets get started," She said as she grabbed a mattress and began to haul it over to her room.

The man, who's name he himself couldn't remember, had moved to this tiny Irish fishing village a few months ago. He lived in a cabin on the far outskirts of town and kept to himself. All the villagers knew of him and had begun calling him Fanai after he had first arrived. No matter his protests, the name had stuck. How he had arrived there and came to be was also something he couldn't entirely remember. His arrival on the island was a scattering of circumstances that were beyond his control. Fanai had awoken a few months ago, as if waking from a bad dream, in a hotel room in the middle of Scotland. His only possessions were a medium sized duffel bag with two changes of clothes, a small toiletries bag, an empty sketchbook, and an assortment of pencils. His wallet, which was stuffed full of cash, also contained a ticket for a 3pm departure on the Belfast Cairnryan ferry.

He neither felt sick, pained, nor hungover. He just felt empty; like he was a vessel delivering a package. When Fanai looked at the ticket he felt something stir inside him, telling him he was supposed to be on that ferry. He felt that if he didn't get onto the ferry, something terrible might happen. It was something far worse than not knowing who he was or why he was there. Looking at his wrist, he discovered a watch, and realized it was already well past one in the afternoon. He got up and realizing he was already fully dressed, thus giving him a third set of clothes. He grabbed his bag, wallet and ticket, and made his way out of the the room.

No one stopped him as he left, nor demanded any money when he dropped the key off at the reception desk. As Fanai walked through the lobby doors a valet pointed him towards a shuttle bus that would take him to the ferry terminal. He had sat down on the bus and it had already pulled away from the hotel, before he realized that he hadn't told the valet where he was going.

The ferry ride was long but beautiful. Fanai sat on the deck, watching the water crest and swell as their ferry chugged its way through. The wind blew heavily around him. It was only then that he noticed he was wearing a heavy jacket, hat and light scarf. He wondered if he had been wearing it when left the hotel. His departure was already becoming a distant past memory.

He pulled out the sketchbook placing it on his lap, took a pencil in his hand and stared off into the distance. He wasn't sure when he started sketching, but by the time the ferry had docked in Ireland he had drawn a rough sketch of a woman's face. She was incredibly beautiful and hauntingly familiar. He was quite certain though, despite his amnesia, that he had never met her before.

When he looked into her eyes, they were filled with an intensely overwhelming sense of sadness, he felt something akin to deja vu. Her eyes were calling to him; searching for him. They held more mystery than his amnesia but he knew that they also held the answers to what he was looking for. Her eyes reminded him of a general in war about to give the order for genocide. She seemed devastated by what was about to transpire. Crushed by the enormity of the despair she was about to bestow not only upon men, but their entire race. He could feel her eyes sucking his soul out of his chest.

He grasped at his jacket furtively; his breath suddenly catching in his throat. Her head began to turn very slowly until her eyes were looking directly into his. She opened her mouth, as if to speak, and a silent scream escaped from her lips. He gasped loudly, sat rigidly upright, his eyes fluttering as he slammed the sketchbook shut. Looking around, he saw that the ferry had docked, that cars were leaving, and he was alone on the deck.

He looked down at the sketchpad and cautiously opened it. He saw her haunting face staring back at him. There were spatters of wet spots on the sketchpad, as if raindrops had fallen upon it. The sky was cloudy but full of sunshine and the air dry. He reached his hand up to his face and upon feeling his cheek he realized it was damp with his tears. He choked back a sob, closing the sketchbook again he shoved it into his duffel bag and ran off the ferry.

Chapter 3

Lian pounded her fist on the door of the bathroom that she and Bruce shared, "Hurry up slowpoke." Lian called out to him.

Bruce grunted from behind the door as Lian pounded on it again. Bruce opened the door, a scowl on his face. Lian held out a cup of coffee and thrust it at him with a bright cheery smile. He took it, grunting again as he took a sip and closed the bathroom door. She sighed and lay down on her bed. She was dressed. Her book bag was full and she had been ready to go for the last two hours. She had made breakfast for both of them and had finished hers more than an hour ago. His was still on her desk, the eggs congealed and the toast soggy. As excited as she was to start class today, she had nervous butterflies in her stomach. The two of them were exchange students starting in their second year of a four year program. The exchange program was still relatively new and they were only the second set of students to go abroad.

Moments later Bruce finally emerged from the bathroom and sauntered towards her, empty coffee mug in hand and still half asleep. She was grateful that he had at least remembered to put his pants on. She held out a croissant and he took a bite from it, mumbling thru a full mouth. She got up, buttoned up his shirt, and tied his tie. He finished the croissant as she refilled his coffee. Seeing the plate of cold eggs, sausage and toast on the desk he frowned. Bruce picked up the sausages and preceded to shove them all into his mouth. She tousled his hair from behind, attempting to spread some gel in it. He turned around to face her, looked her over top to bottom and nodded approvingly. She did a little twirl and curtsied as he grinned, giving her two thumbs up. They both had on the university's second year uniform. Each program at the university was represented by a specific uniform that were literally straight out of a Japanese manga series. Bruce wore navy blue slacks, a white short sleeve shirt, and a short navy blue tie. He also had an optional pullover vest that became mandatory in the wintertime. She wore a navy blue pleated skirt that rode dangerously high as far as he was concerned, a white form fitting blouse and a navy blue tie around her neck. She also wore a matching navy blue headband and her hair was tied back in a loose braid. They both had optional navy blue jackets that bore their program and year's emblem on it. Lian pranced about the room until he finished shoving food in his face. Bruce picked up his bag and held the door open as the two of them left the dorm together.

They stood on the doorstep, their dorm located directly outside one of many entrances to the university. It was a collection of massive buildings that had been built over the course of a hundred years ago and had been carefully maintained over the years. Lian tugged at Bruce's sleeve and he looked down at her. She mouthed the word 'wow' and he nodded in agreement. Their own university back home was maybe a third of this size and they were sure there were even more buildings that they couldn't yet see. She pulled out the campus map and consulted it. After a bit of discussion they headed towards their first class.

The scenery on the walk was breathtaking. Bruce felt like she was walking thru a movie set. The grounds were decorated like a large Japanese garden with bonsai trees, sakura blossom trees, and a variety of other Japanese flora. They were all perfectly pruned and appealing to the eye. They filled every nook and cranny as far as the eye could see. There were even mini temples and shrines complete with water fountains and tiny incense burning platforms. If not for the large mountains in the background she would have thought they were in her native country of Japan and she felt an immediate affinity to the campus. Other students had uniforms similar to theirs. The variations between them were subtle enough to give the impression of uniformity while still clearly marking their differences. Lian crossed her hands over her chest and shivered with happiness and excitement.

She found their first classroom and poked her head inside. It was a large auditorium, akin to the ones back home. Seats raked upwards and out in a semi circle that surrounded a small lectern for the professor. There was a desk below the chalkboard and a ten foot by ten foot floor space surrounding the lectern. They were still quite early yet the classroom was already half full. Lian took a deep breath but before she could exhale Bruce pushed her into the classroom. She stumbled through the door. Bruce reached out, caught her by the elbow and steadied her. She continued into the classroom her face now beet red and Bruce followed, aloof and indifferent as usual. She could feel the students stare, eyeing the obvious newbies to their program. Lian walked up to the middle of the auditorium and took a seat near the aisle. Bruce followed, the guys quickly dismissing him and the girls already gawking over him. She smiled, knowing that Bruce was good looking and that attention followed him wherever he went. Not only was he attractive, but he was incredibly smart and a strong athlete. He could have easily received a full football scholarship to any university of his choice. Lian tried not to laugh at all of the attention he received, knowing that he never really cared about the fake adoration. That he preferred women with substance and hated the shallow interest he typically got.

Bruce sat down beside Lian and she leaned over to whisper into his ear, "You don't have to sit with me if you don't want to."

Bruce whispered in her ear, "And let the wolves get me? Just how cruel are you?" He laughed as he patted her leg.

She fought back a laugh herself as she pulled out her notebook and pencil case, automatically handing Bruce a pen when he held his hand out for one. He grunted appreciation and put the pen behind his ear. The classroom quickly filled up as the professor came in and set his bag in the lectern. He pulled out a large stack of papers and set them next his bag. He cleared his throat and everyone in the class quieted down, giving him their full attention. The professor smiled and looked up at his students.

"As most of you already know, my name is Richard Meer. Today we welcome two exchange students into our program. Their names are..." he flipped through his notebook and scrolled a finger down the page, "Lian Tremblay and Bruce Burrows." He scanned the auditorium, "Please rise."

Lian looked over uncomfortably at Bruce who was already standing. He shrugged his shoulders and waved his hand like the queen. A few of the students chuckled. He tugged at her arm and pulled her to her feet. She gave a brief wave while her face turned beet red and quickly sat back down .

"You're from Canada, correct?" the professor asked and Bruce replied with a yes that was more grunt than yes. "Good, good. These two students," he started, addressing the remainder of the classroom, "not only excel in their academics and come highly recommended from Winston University, but they both received the Star of Life award last year for their heroic efforts in saving the occupants of a small elderly home that burst into flames. We welcome you here from the bottom of our hearts. I hope you find our humble establishment to your liking."

The class burst into applause and Bruce mockingly clutched his hands together and swung them in the air like a victor while Lian continued to blush, shrinking further into her seat. She was not used to this kind of attention and loathed it.

The professor waved the noise down with a single motion, "This is one of two classes that all of the students are required to take in the paramedical program. The remainder of your classes will be more specialized in your area of expertise and desire. Today we will merely go over the expectations of the year."

Handouts mysteriously appeared and spread themselves amongst the students. Bruce took two and handed one to Lian. The professor continued to drone on, explaining his expectations for them, how to utilize the facility and new privileges only open to second year students. Lian focused all of her energy into taking notes and paying close attention to the professor. She felt her hand begin to shake slightly, so she reached into her bag and snuck a couple of pills into her mouth. Bruce leaned back and absorbed the facts. Despite his laid back demeanour he was actually a great student. He could simply retain everything he heard.

Once the class was over they had an hour until their next class together so they decided to explore the campus. They had just gotten outside the building when a group of students, possibly even the same ones who ransacked their dorm rooms, crashed into them. One of the girls giggled and handed them a flyer. Lian took it and saw that it had an address and a phone number on it.

"Big party tonight in your honour. BYOB. Don't be late!" one of them shouted as they continued on, handing out flyers to all the students on campus. Lian tried to thank them but they ran off too quickly. She looked at it, showed it to Bruce, and they both smiled.

Bruce and Lian walked quietly outside, enjoying the fresh mountain air. Their morning classes had flown by in a flash. Lian studied her schedule, noting that her next class was without Bruce. She felt a little nervous but scolded herself. He wasn't even supposed to be here with her. She had applied on her own hoping to give Bruce the break from her he needed and deserved. But, he had surprised her by applying himself and getting accepted in the same program as herself. She had then secretly hoped that they would be together for all of their classes like they had been in high school.

Realistically Lian knew that despite being in the same program it was unlikely that they would be in all the same classes. The university boasted highly specialized and diverse classes. One could learn much more in a specific area of almost any area of expertise. It was also the excuse Bruce gave her after showing her his acceptance letter. Here paramedics were given the opportunity to learn more about becoming doctors and encouraged to be more involved with their patients outside of just the ambulance. That drew Lian's interest greatly, although she knew that it was unlikely she'd ever progress to becoming a doctor. Bruce, on the other hand, had a keen interest in the science and research courses that they offered. His course load was much heavier than hers and he had to request permission to exceed the regular course load in order to take on three extra courses per semester. He was currently doing it on a trial basis and would be permitted to continue the extra course load if he passed the first term with flying colours. If not, he would have to drop them and stick with a regular course load.

Lian sat down on a bench, stifled a yawn, and stretched. She was still jet lagged and her body ached like the devil. The dorm beds were not as comfortable as her usual firm futon back home. They were definitely worn in, overly soft and lumpy.

Bruce returned with two lattes in hand and she eagerly took hers. As quickly as she gulped down her first sip she spat it back out and waved her hand like a fan in front of her mouth, waggling her burnt tongue.

Bruce laughed and ruffled her hair, "Whatcha thinking about silly chicken?" he said as she glared at him. She hated that nickname. He'd been calling her that since they were six.

She stared out in front of her wistfully, "Just wondering if we made the right choice coming here."

"Having doubts?" he asked. She shook her head slowly from side to side as if still trying to convince herself.

A couple of cute guys in uniforms marked with a red crest, walked by and whistled as they saw Lian. She smiled shyly and waved back at them. They came over to her and the four of them began to chat. The guys quickly left Bruce out of the conversation, peppering Lian with questions about herself. Bruce abruptly got to his feet and walked away. Lian immediately jumped to her feet, knocking her still open book bag to the ground and spilling everything out of it. The guys looked at her awkwardly and walked away. Lian called out to Bruce as she knelt down to pick up her books, but he was already too far away to hear her. A hand reached out of nowhere and helped her pick up her books.

"Thank you," Lian said as she stuffed the last book into her bag.

The hand reached out again, took hers, and pulled her to her feet. She smiled and looked up to see Adonis. Not the actual greek god Adonis, but a close enough facsimile; or perhaps, his reincarnation. The man before her was tall with long, wavy, dirty blonde hair. He was lean, muscular, and had the deepest blue eyes she had ever seen. He leaned in close and lightly kissed both of her cheeks. Her face flushed over and he apologized. He shook her hand as he introduced himself. Lian mumbled her name back as she shook his hand. He smiled and excused himself before heading back into the depths of the campus. He had only taken a few steps when he turned on his heels, came back, taking both her hands in his.

"You are coming to this party tonight, yes?" he asked her. Lian could only nod in answer. He said, "My name is Darin, pleasure to meet you Lian," with a smile. He gave her another peck on the cheek and jogged off.

It took a few moments before she realized that her Adonis had left, that Bruce was nowhere in sight and that she was drooling. She sighed, wiped the drool off of her face and wondered if she had done something to put Bruce off. She pulled out her map, confirmed her location, and started off towards her next class.

The house was insanely huge. It looked more like a miniature mansion mixed with a chalet than a house. Apparently, houses like these were quite common this far up the mountain. From the outside, it looked like the party was already in full swing. Music was blaring through the windows, lights flickered throughout the house and students were draped everywhere you could imagine and also few places you wouldn't. Bruce and Lian walked up a small cobblestone path and onto the porch, this afternoon's interactions long forgotten. She held a bottle of wine and a cheese tray, while he had a six pack of beer.

Lian looked up at Bruce, her eyes flickering with nervousness, "Are you sure we want to do this?" She smiled meekly, knowing she had to go but also equally wanting to be in her room, curled up with a good book. Or any book really.

Bruce grabbed her shoulders and rubbed them vigorously, "Awww, c'mon. Don't be such a spoilsport. They threw it just for us."

"I'm not a spoilsport, I'm just tired. There's this thing called jet lag. Maybe you've heard of it?" Lian said with a pout, "And they used us an excuse to throw the party. Let's be real. If we weren't here, I'm sure they'd have found another good reason for it."

"Thats my girl, always the optimist," Bruce laughed as he pushed his way through the ajar front door. They were met with even louder music and endless amounts of smoke. Her eyes stung as they welled up with water. She coughed, waving a hand in front of her face. Bruce gave her a look of sympathy and tried to wave the smoke away from her.

In the far corner of the main room Darin saw them enter. With a big smile on his face he stepped through a group of girls and interrupted their conversation. They were angry at first but when they saw whom he was referring to they quickly forgave him and rushed over to greet Bruce. Lian received a frosty hello from one girl who then proceeded to wedge herself between her and Bruce, bumping Lian out of the way. The girls began to giggle and fawn over Bruce as one of them took him by the arm and lead him away, further into the depths of the house. Lian barely had time to process what was happening as they were already disappearing. Bruce managed to wave a hand in her direction. Lian just shrugged her shoulders and smiled.

If they could manage to keep Bruce occupied, she would be able to sneak off earlier than originally anticipated. It had been Bruce's idea to come to the party. He had insisted that the girls had invited them both, which they had, and that it was an party open to all. Based on the sheer number of students she could see, it probably was. She had wanted to stay home and study, but he had accused her of being a nerd and told her that she needed to lighten up. When Lian had insisted on staying home, he had refused to go to the party without her. She had known that he would skip the party just to annoy her all evening, thus thwarting any attempts to study. So she gave in with the hopes of ditching him as soon as she possibly could.

The throng of people in front of her looked difficult to navigate through, but Lian saw no other way towards, where she thought, was the kitchen. She needed a glass for her wine and wanted to drop off the cheese tray somewhere safe. She pushed her way through and was rewarded with not only the kitchen but a fairly empty one at that. One could actually navigate themselves quite easily through it.

The kitchen, much like the exterior, was also overwhelming in size. There were three large refrigerators along the one wall, a large six element gas stove and an even larger island in the centre of the room. The cupboards were white with a teal blue seaside like design that was soft and subtle. What wall that did show between the counters and cupboards were matching teal tiles with white undertones.

There was an assortment of chips, dips and other easy to grab snacks scattered on the island. Two couples were making out on a bench across from it. Each couple either oblivious of the other or more likely, just not caring. There were several large red plastic dixie cups on the counters, a variety of soda and hard liquors. One student opened the middle fridge to reveal a wall of beer.

No one took notice of her as she entered the kitchen or acknowledged her as she sashayed her way to the island. Lian put her cheese tray down and unwrapped it. She grabbed a dixie cup, opened her wine, poured herself a generous portion, and took a large sip.

"Are all Canadians that bold with their wine?" a voice from behind asked her.

Lian looked over the edge of her cup and saw Darin, the adonis she had met earlier that day. Her eyes twinkled as she took in his chiseled chin and the rippling of his biceps. "I'm probably the wimpiest drinker in my country."

"I find that hard to believe. You went after that wine like a champ."

Lian laughed. "A well deserved reward for battling my way through this crowd. Would you like a glass?" she asked, offering him the bottle. He held up a can of beer and shook his head no.

"Would you like to go somewhere, a little less crowded?" he asked her. He made his way beside her and gingerly placed a hand on her lower back.

She smiled and nodded. He held his hand more firmly on her back and guided her thru the crowd with ease towards the back of the kitchen where he revealed a hidden staircase. It was narrower than an ordinary staircase and was only wide enough for a single person to pass. He stepped up the staircase first and held a hand out for her. As she took it he looked out across the kitchen and saw Bruce. He gave him a giant grin as he took Lian's hand and led her up the stairs. Bruce dashed across the kitchen only to be stopped midway by yet another group of girls all wanting his attention. He watched helplessly as Lian and Darin disappeared.

They emerged on the second floor in a small room that was once used by the servants of the original household owners back when it had been first built, but had since been repurposed into a pantry. There was still some old furniture in the corner and Darin pulled out a small sofa. He brushed the dust off of it and sat down. He patted the empty seat next to him and a cloud of dust sprung to life. Hesitantly she sat down beside him. They sat together in silence, Darin patiently waiting while Lian scoured the contents of the pantry.

"How did you know?" she asked.

Darin chuckled, "I'm training to be a profiler, I'd be embarrassed if I couldn't read you so easily."

In a huff she jumped to her feet, "Oh, so I'm easy to read am I?"

He grabbed her hand, "That's not what I meant. I'm sorry that came out all wrong," he started, looking her straight in the eyes. "What I meant is that it's obvious to see when someone is uncomfortable. Not you per say."

Lian sighed and let him pull her back down to the couch, "I've never been good with people, not like Bruce is."

"He is quite the charmer isn't he?" Darin said carefully.

She laughed softly, "Since we were kids. He could sweet talk himself out of any trouble we got ourselves into."

"You are, childhood friends then?"

Lian nodded, "Yup, since we were babies."

"So then the two of you, aren't ..." he said letting his voice trail off.

"Aren't what?" she asked suspiciously.

"An item?"

Lian looked at him, the seriousness in his eyes and burst out laughing.

Darin looked at her skeptically, "Did I say something funny? Is my english that bad?"

She wiped the tears from her eyes as she regained her composure, "No, no, not at all. But I've only just realized that's probably why everyone is looking at us funny. Everyone must assume that we're a couple. Back home, since we grew up together in a fairly small city, everyone knew we were like brother and sister. No one questioned our closeness. But here, we're strangers. No wonder the girls keep giving me death looks."

He slid closer to her on the couch and gently placed his muscular arm around her shoulders, "Well that is good news for me then," Darin said as he leaned in to kiss her.

"What do you-" Lian started but abruptly stopped when she realized his face was incredibly close to hers. Even up close he appeared flawless. She put a hand between their mouths and got up from the couch, "I'm sorry. This is just a bit too fast for me."

She ran off towards the stairs and dashed down. From the couch he chuckled with a sly smile on his lips, "I do like a challenge."

Lian burst into the kitchen and ran through it. She felt her face growing hot as she ran into the adjoining room. She saw another staircase and ran up it. It was relatively empty and a good spot to be seen by Bruce. Lian gingerly touched her lips before she looked up and realized that everyone was looking at her and not in a good way. She could feel their eyes staring her down like miniature ice daggers. The girls were either visibly snubbing her or shooting her dirty looks while the guys were undressing her with their eyes. The odd unlucky guy would get a jab to his ribcage if caught peeping at Lian. Their cattiness reminded her of the high school drama she had hoped to leave behind.

Halfway up the staircase Lian found a small nook in the wall. She ducked into it sighing a breath of relief. She could hide out there briefly, away from the crowd, and take a moment to recover. She closed her eyes and leaned up against the wall, trying to burrow herself deep within it. The sound of familiar voices caught her attention. She realized a small group of her classmates were only a bit further up the stairs from her. She could only make out small snippets of their conversation, but they were complaining about something or someone.

Lian heard, "stuck up . . . think they're smarter than us . . .

girlfriend stealing . . .useless Canadians." Her breath drew in sharply and she slapped her hands over her mouth. She knew, that for whatever reason, she wasn't well liked but had just chalked it up to being an outsider. She hadn't expected this much hatred, especially given that they had only been there a couple of days. She had assumed that everyone in her program did well academically as it was incredibly difficult for both her and Bruce to get enrolled in this specific program.

Subconsciously, Lian leaned in closer and heard that they were complaining about the exchange system and how the university should have never let their program become a part of it. That doing so meant foreigners could steal their jobs. One of the biggest reasons she wanted to come to this university was it had a higher post graduate to job ratio. From what she could overhear, very few graduates ended up with their ideal job. Most became regular paramedics and only those in the top five percent ever got the *gravy jobs*. Lian had never thought about the implications the two of them succeeding well academically would do to the others. Neither she nor Bruce wanted the gravy jobs they talked about. She wanted to be regular paramedic and Bruce wasn't even likely to remain a paramedic. His original desire was to become a researcher. She had presumed that since the students here got most of the better jobs in Europe, that had meant overall the program was more intense and that they would learn more here than anywhere else. She had never considered the idea of stealing someone else's job.

The guys began to complain about Bruce stealing all of the girls attention while the girls complained about Lian's superior attitude. That she was only pretending to be modest and shy. That she had Bruce on a leash and wouldn't have even made it into the program without his help. They said that the only reason Lian had been granted enrolment was because Bruce insisted upon it. Lian's heart lurched with anger and her hands clenched tightly. Blatant lies and stupid jealousy, she thought. She had gotten accepted at the university before Bruce even applied for it himself. Not that telling them now would matter. They would believe their lies over her truth without a forethought.

Unable to listen anymore she pushed herself away from the wall, dropping her cup to the floor, wine flying everywhere. Someone yelled out as the wine splashed on their pants, but she didn't pay attention. She had already made her way up the remainder of the staircase, past the gossipers, and away from the crowd.

At the bottom of the stairs Bruce saw her and tried to follow, but one of the girls nearby grabbed his arm and squeezed it tightly, cooing about how he must work out a lot. His face immediately went flush and he forgot what had distracted him a moment ago.

Lian made her way into the first empty room she could find and closed the door behind her. She fell down onto the bed face first and screamed. When she finally felt like she had let it all out and had regained some control, she sat up. She could hear muffled whispers in the room next to her. Someone was going at it pretty hot and heavy in the next room. She went back to the door and cracked it open. Before she could step through it she heard another group of girls talking about her. They were whispering about how she had just run up there, obviously crushed that Bruce was popular and that she wasn't. That they were surprised she had even bothered to show up at the party and how she was just a waste of space.

Slowly Lian closed the door, leaned her back against it, slid down and tried to hold back the tears. She looked up and saw sliding patio doors at the far end of the room. She got to her feet and dashed across the room at almost a full sprint;

opening the patio door she stepped outside. The air was crisp and unseasonably warm for September. A glance below showed the backyard was as full of students as the inside of the house was. She slumped down until she was seated on the floor of the patio and hugging her knees to her chest, cried.

Chapter 4

It was already noon and Lian was in much better spirits than she had been the last couple of weeks. Jumping up and down, she waved her hands frantically. Bruce chuckled, knowing that she had probably found yet another cute animal and was wanting to show it off to him. He had already watched her pull out her camera and take several pictures of him slowly approaching her in attempts to get his attention. Slinging the camera over her shoulder, Lian put her hands on her hips, glaring at him while impatiently tapping her foot. He held his hands out in front of him taking a mock picture of her and she stuck her tongue out at him. Smiling Bruce jogged over towards her as she resumed her picture taking.

When he finally caught up with Lian he found she was holding a small bird in one hand. The bird was a soft creamy white with speckles of metallic gold flakes in its feathers. It glistened in the sunlight as it hopped about in her hand and up her forearm. The smile on Lian's face made his heart jump into his throat. He made a conscious effort to calm himself before he touched her hand gently, allowing the bird to hop onto his hand. Strangely enough the bird seemed to lose some of its sparkle once in his hands. Lian noticed this and tried to reposition his hands in the sunlight better. She sighed as the bird, finally bored, flew away.

Lian continued up the trail, turning back briefly to inquire about lunch. Bruce shrugged his shoulders and she bounded off like a deer in search of a nice place to eat. She found a small clearing that overlooked the valley below them. From her backpack she pulled out a blanket and laid it neatly on the ground. Quickly and efficiently she set out a large array of cold cuts, cheese, nuts, berries, a baguette and a thermos of coffee mixed with a bit of cocoa. She also set out a Tupperware of assorted Swiss treats including chocolate. When she finished laying everything out Lian looked up to find Bruce enjoying the view before them.

She gazed fondly at Bruce's back. Part of her heart raced when she caught herself gazing at him. She could feel her face begin to flush as she allowed her mind to wander to what could be. She knew that Bruce adored her; much more than just friends. Even though Bruce had yet to say anything to her directly. His actions spoke much louder than words each and every day. She knew that he had yet to have a girlfriend; not even in high school. The two of them were so joined at the hip that no one in school dared to try and part them. Lian often wondered why Bruce had never asked for more or why he had never made any physical advances towards her. But while she wondered about this she was also extremely grateful. In the earlier years of high school she was sure she would have jumped at the opportunity to be his girlfriend, but by grade eleven something inside her had changed. She wasn't sure exactly what had happened, but by the time she had turned sixteen a feeling inside her started to push him away from her romantically. So she had decided to pursue the paramedical services field simply because Lian knew that Bruce wanted to become a researcher and it should have separated them enough academically. Lian knew that she would be able to finish her schooling much earlier than Bruce and therefore be able to separate herself more easily.

What Lian didn't understand was why she suddenly felt the way she did. She was still attracted to him - wildly so. Not a moment went by where she didn't want to be with him. Lian knew that she was in love with Bruce. But something inside herself told her to keep distance from him. The more she listened to the voice inside the more she felt it was meant to be a brotherly type love. Lian felt that being with him was a very dangerous prospect for him, as she knew that she wasn't long for this world. Something big was about to happen to her and she was terribly afraid of how it would hurt him. So despite how she felt, she did her best to keep him at bay.

But Bruce knew her better than she did herself and had changed his career path to be with her. When he learned that Lian had secretly applied to a school abroad, unbeknownst to her he too applied. She knew that the main reason he had gotten accepted was that he presented the two of them as a pair and that the university they were now attending had wanted to send a couple in exchange to study in Canada.

Bruce turned around, a giant grin on his face, and waved her over. Lian feigned boredom and popped a piece of cheese into her mouth. He reluctantly joined her on the blanket and she fed him a piece of cheese. They ate in relative silence, enjoying the music of the birds, the gentle rustling of leaves that played in the background and the soft scuttling of animals moving about. Once finished their meal Lian began cleaning up while Bruce pulled out his own camera to photograph the scenery. When she finished she looked up to discover that Bruce had disappeared. His camera bag, however, was still on the ground nearby. Lian called out to him and thought she heard a muffled reply from just over the edge.

She went to the edge and peered over. There, almost twenty feet below her, was Bruce, snapping away like a mad man. Lian rolled her eyes and called down to Bruce. He begged for a few more minutes and she begrudgingly agreed. She lay down on the ground, her head on his camera bag and shouted out that he had five minutes max before she would leave him behind.

An eagle cried as it soared in the sky above her. A lone pirate in the endless sea that was the sky. Lian consulted her watch and called out to Bruce, telling him to hustle his butt. He shouted back that he was coming and she could hear him grunt as he scaled back up the mountain. The sudden sound of rocks falling followed by a loud thud and then silence immediately brought her to her feet. Lian looked over the edge but could no longer see him.

"Bruce?" Lian called out frantically, afraid that she had just heard him fall, "Bruce?! Where are you?".

There was no answer as the seconds ticked by slowly. She looked over the cliff edge and still saw nothing. She called out to Bruce again, unsure of what to do. Pulling out her phone Lian discovered she had no service. She frowned, knowing it would take a couple of hours before she could reach anyone by foot.

She called out again when a hand slapped the ground beside her foot. She crouched down and saw that Bruce was injured. His pants were torn and blood was seeping out near his ankle. She reached out and grabbed his arm, pulling him up over the edge. He groaned in pain as he rolled onto the ground nursing his left ankle.

"Bruce what happened?"

Embarrassed, Bruce reluctantly admitted that he had stopped mid climb to take a picture of the eagle. He then slipped, twisting his ankle. It scraped along the mountain before he landed on the ledge. Lian pulled him to his feet and watched as he tried to put weight on his ankle. He immediately winced in pain as it made contact with the ground. She helped him to a seated position before pulling her first aid kit out of his bag.

Sprain aside, the injury was mostly superficial. The blood probably smeared as he fell, making it look worse than it really was. Lian first donned gloves then proceeded to clean and bandage the wound. Looking inside her kit she debated on whether she should bandage his ankle or try to splint it. Absently she started moving her hands over his ankle, gently tracing her fingers along his skin, momentarily lost in her thoughts. Bruce grew quiet as one hand rested on his injured ankle and the other rummaged thru the first aid kit. As she looked for the tensor bandage Bruce gasped softly. Lian told him to stop being such a wimp as she tossed the tensor bandage at his face. She didn't notice that a soft white light was emanating from her hand to his ankle. She was still looking for the clips to hold the tensor bandage. She turned back to face him, holding out her hand to him. Bruce looked as his ankle, the light now gone and wondered if he had just imagined the whole thing. Yet he couldn't wipe the shocked look off of his face.

"Earth to Bruce. Bandage?"

He reached into his lap, picked up the tensor bandage and gingerly placed it into her hand. "You didn't see that, did you?" he asked her.

"See what." she said as she unwrapped the plastic on the tensor bandage and began to wrap his ankle. When she finished she used the clips to hold it close, pulled his sock onto his foot, and helped him put his boot back on. She looked pleasantly surprised when his boot went on with little resistance, "Oh good, there doesn't appear to be much swelling." She proclaimed proudly.

Bruce looked back at his ankle and then at Lian, who was now standing up and holding a hand out to him.

"Are you going to stare at me all day?" Lian asked, eyeing him skeptically.

He took her hand and let her pull him up and onto to his one foot. He tapped the ground lightly with his left foot and felt no pain. "You really didn't see anything, did you?"

"See what? My hands? Your ankle?" Lian asked with a laugh, "Why are you being so mysterious?"

Bruce shook his head and put all of his weight onto his left ankle, "No reason, I guess. Lets just go home."

Lian watched him move about easily, "Did a better job than I thought. Are you good to walk?" she asked him.

He nodded yes, looking off into the distance, a puzzled look on his face.

A planet in the far reaches of the Universe

The tavern was low lit and loud. Despite the early hour, it was bustling with life and quite crowded. Along with the usual tables and barstools strewn about it possessed a wall of booths. Some hidden in the far depths of the back and dressed with curtains for those who required discretion. In one of these booths the seven of them sat. Their voices were hushed but hurried.

"We're dying. What was the point of going to all that trouble if we're still going to die?" the Eldrossian said.

"He's right, I don't want to die unexpectedly," the Sawain said, drumming his fingers nervously on the table, "The crystals were supposed to prolong our lives. A few thousand years wasn't worth the risk."

The others nodded in agreement. The Dragonian sat in the very back with Darelbaiden on one side and the Remkin on the other side. The Remkin looked from side to side, nervously inching away from Darelbaiden, who looked ready to kill them all in an instant.

"Calling us here was foolish and even more risky than the initial operation," Darelbaiden proclaimed, his voice icy and full of rage.

"Dammit, I don't want my people dying! I did this for them," The Remkin exclaimed and the whole group turned to face him with surprise. His race was known for their docile nature, not their boldness. "If they've hadn't figured out who we are by now, they never will…… Its been long enough," His face was bright red and his eyes darted about, flickering in the low lighting. The rest of the group stared at him flustered. He squirmed in his seat and mumbled that he had nothing more to say.

The Dragonion cleared his throat and everyone turned to face him. As they did the Remkin breathed a sigh of relief. "We may have come up with a solution," He stated and was met with looks of overwhelming disbelief from everyone.

"Go on." The Eldrossian said.

The Dragonion proceeded to explain how he had shared his portion not only with his family, but with the elders and wisest on his planet. That he did so in order to utilize their intelligence and experience to find ways to prolong their lives more naturally. To discover a way to expand the crystal's resources before it was fully expended. Despite the others being of good health, one of the elders had reached his final stages of life with his mind, body and soul showing signs of decay. His scales turned bright red and had begun to flake off like dried skin.

The Dragonian told them how at this point one usually takes up their most inner demons and casts them aside to make peace with their enemies and rejoice with their loved ones. That they will often travel throughout their own village and the neighbouring ones, if their body permits, to pay their respects. During such a journey this particular dying elder came to one of his oldest enemies. He too was on his deathbed. In the visit the enemy had begged for forgiveness. He pleaded, blaming the misery he had caused on youthful arrogance. To show how much he had been pained by his own betrayal he took his blade and slit his own throat, dying in the visiting elder's arms. And in that moment, as death overtook him, his soul escaped from his body and went into the visiting elders body. When that happened his scales were restored back to their original vibrant green, his youth restored. This newfound youth however only lasted a few years and when the elder was once again struck with decay he went out to the forest, found a fox and its young nestled deep within a brush. He slaughtered them all and youth was once again bestowed upon him. This was over twenty years ago and he had remained ever young since.

They looked at each other carefully. The words that Dragonion spoke wore heavy on their hearts. He had indeed, albeit unintentionally, found a solution, but at what cost? Was it really something that they were prepared to do? They sat in silence staring numbly at each other. Their faces began to flush with embarrassment and their eyes danced about nervously.

Darelbaiden spoke first, "So, killing lower life forms satisfies it?" he asked and the Dragonion nodded his head eagerly. "Can't really see a problem with that, can we? If we kill to eat, then we also kill to live, right?" the others slowly nodded in agreement.

"As long as we draw the line there," the Nomda said, staring everyone firmly in the eye, "then there shouldn't be any concern."

The others nodded eagerly. They were unaware of how quickly that line would approach them, or how easily they would cross it.

The library, like most, was filled to the brim with books. What made this one unique was its architecture. Some no name designer had won the bid for the design and proceeded to bring forth a design that blew everyone completely out of the water. His popularity grew immensely after the contest and he became known as an 'open air conceptualist'. The main floor was large and open with several staircases flowing in upward spirals to a variety of interconnecting landings on second and third levels. The main floor was like a loft, that was heavily divided yet open. Sections of the main floor had transparent metal and glass ceilings. The main support was intricately designed metal mesh embedded in glass. The most upper ceiling was also glass. When you looked up, depending on where you stood, your gaze was met with variations of sunlight dancing through the ceilings. It had an intriguingly, quaint, British feeling to it.

There were two spiral staircases from the first floor that went all the way to the third floor bypassing the second floor entirely. It too, was open, but much more so than the second floor. Access to these staircases required a keycard only obtainable from one of the librarians, who did not hand them out willy nilly. The third floor sections contained special resources books that could not be checked out. In these two sections on opposite sides of the room, where lounges set up for ease of reading and note taking.

From the second floor there were several staircases that spiralled up to the central area of the third floor. Each to a separate landing, these ones were easily accessible by anyone. Each landing was yet another topic of literature or reference material. Each contained books you could check out.

The outer walls, like the ceilings, were a combination of glass and metal work laced with intricate designs. The glass was tinted ever so slightly to prevent UV rays from damaging the books inside. It allowed for enough natural light that there was only a minimal amount of indoor lighting needed during the daytime. Overall, it was an immaculate, breathtaking and beautiful library.

Part of the admissions package included the names of several apps to download onto you phone or tablet, including one that allowed you to navigate the library. You either entered a topic, genre or actual name of book or author and the app routed you to where you needed to go within the library; much like a GPS tracker. You could then see if the book you needed was in, when it would be returned if it was out, and alternative book options. The app was designed by a student in the technology program a year prior. Bruce typed in the name of a medical researcher he had been hunting and instantly it popped up with several research papers. Guiding him to the elusive third floor landing.

Up there he found only a few students milling about. The topics in this section were highly specialized medical reports and research. His fellow dorm mates had talked about how rare it was for anyone to ever go up there. By the way they talked about it he got the impression that only big nerds and those with insanely high GPA's ever went up there. Which was perfect for him. Bruce discovered that there was an endless collection of medical journals and research papers on a variety of diseases and illnesses. He knew that there wasn't a cure for what he was looking for, but had hoped to find either an avenue that someone had overlooked or research papers not available or known in Canada. A large part of him wanted to attend this school not only for the courses in medical research, but also the resources the school claimed to have. Bruce was happy to see that they stood up to their reputation. He pulled out a few medical journals the app suggested and sat down in a small orange lounge chair. He opened his notebook on his lap and held a pen in his hand.

"Autosomal dominant disorder? Thats a mouthful for a paramedic isn't it?" a voice said from behind him.

Bruce lowered the journal and turned to see Darin, the good looking blonde guy that had been hitting on Lian weeks earlier. He grunted and turned back to his journal. Darin grabbed his shoulders and began to rub them more vigorously than Bruce felt comfortable with. He tried to ignore Darin and continue with his reading.

"This got anything to do with that hot girl I saw you with? What was her name, Lynne?"

Bruce lowered the journal into his lap, "What do you want?" he asked through gritted teeth.

Darin walked around the chair and sat down next to Bruce, "A do over. I've obviously infringed upon your territory and I want to apologize." He held out his hand and Bruce begrudgingly shook it, "Name is Darin."

Bruce lowered his hand into his lap, he could feel his defences crumbling, "Bruce. Pleased to meet you. And its Lian."

Darin looked at him confused, "Lian?"

"The hot girl. Her name is Lian," Bruce mumbled, hating his Canadian politeness at the moment.

"Ah yes, your girlfriend."

Bruce went to correct Darin but stopped himself. He figured that no harm could come from this guy not knowing the truth. Bruce smiled and nodded his head.

"She's awfully friendly for someone who is taken, I must admit," Darin said with a sly smile on his lips.

Bruce felt himself beginning to tense up, "I don't own her. She's free to do whatever she pleases," He said almost too quickly.

"And whomever?"

Bruce slammed his books shut loudly and sat upright, his

back stiff, "I don't appreciate what you're implying."

Darin slapped his shoulder and laughed aloud, "You're too easy to rile up mate, you need to relax a little."

Bruce let out a breath through gritted teeth but scolded himself internally. He knew better. He was better. Yet he couldn't help himself; not when it came to her.

Darin rubbed Bruce's shoulder again, "I'm sorry, that was in poor taste, wasn't it?"

Bruce shook his head and mumbled something about being too gullible.

"But she is popular, isn't she? You can see heads turn whenever she walks by. You are one lucky man," Darin said and Bruce tried to smile fondly, but it was filled with sadness. "If I were you, I'd never let her out of my sight. Us Swiss men are all animals, I wouldn't trust us. Someone is bound to pounce on her sometime soon."

Bruce looked perplexed, "I trust her," He said hesitantly.

"That's good of you. I know I wouldn't be able to contain myself if I were you. We share a class on Wednesdays and not only is she the prettiest thing in the whole class, but she's also the only girl there. Her smile lights up the room for us wolves and we just lap it up." He leaned in closer to Bruce, his eyes dancing. Bruce swallowed deeply. "I mean, if she's yours, then obviously she's just making polite small talk. But she's always chatting with all the guys in the class. They surround her the second she shows up. She's always smiling, flirting, batting those dark, luscious, eyelashes. Those eyes of hers, they could eat you up whole. And when she touches your arm, you can't help but get chills that run down your whole body. But, you trust her, so obviously, you've nothing to worry about, right?" Darin said with a giant wolfish grin on his face.

Bruce just nodded numbly. Darin quickly got up and waved a hand. "Gotta go, class is about to start, I wouldn't want to miss my chance to chat with your girl," He said, over emphasizing the word 'your.' Darin disappeared into the aisles, leaving Bruce sitting alone in his chair, his mind reeling.

Chapter 5

Bruce ran down the field, the crowd cheering him on as cheerleaders shouted his name in full force. The ball came spiralling towards him and he ducked to the right, just slipping free of the blocking defensive player. As he caught the ball with seconds left in the game, he found himself in the clear and ran towards end zone with only a few yards left to go.

As Bruce crossed the goal line, the crowd erupted with screams and he fell to his knees, kissing the ball before standing up. Arms outstretched he held the ball high, revelling in the adoration of the crowd. As he turned the crowd grew eerily silent and vanished into thin air. The ball slid out of his hand and hit the ground silently, dissolving into the turf. Bruce slowly lowered his arms looking at the empty field, trying to make sense of what had just happened. He had just scored the winning touchdown for the Super Bowl championship. So where had everyone gone?

Bruce walked across the field towards the bleachers that should have been full of his fans. His walk quickly became a jog and then a full on sprint. The field continued to grow beneath his feet. Bruce felt himself getting further and further away. The bleachers quickly became a tiny speck off in the distance. He stopped and scratched his head realizing that he wasn't wearing his helmet anymore. When had he taken it off? He looked down at his hands and found them both empty.

Bruce turned around to see where he could have dropped it, surprised to find an older couple close to his parents age standing right behind him. Startled, he jumped and fell to the ground, landing on his butt. Shaken, he looked up and studied them closely as they stared expectantly, yet silently at him. They were both in their late forties with long dark brown hair with a reddish tinge. The man wore his in a loose ponytail with a tiny braid whipped around, like a vine growing up it. The woman wore hers loose and pulled back at the sides. Their eyes were the deepest blue-green he had ever seen, like he was staring at the inner depths of the ocean and he could feel himself getting lost in them. They both wore long tunics that rested just below their knees. Underneath the tunics were loose fitting pants ending above their ankles. They were incredibly pale, albino like, and they glowed ever so slightly, flickering like a light bulb that was about to die.

They stared at him with soft smiles, that quickly turned into frowns. Their eyes met in a way that appeared to be deep in thought with each other. Bruce could see the questioning concern in her eyes and the man's nod of approval. They turned to face him again and he realized that he was no longer in his football jersey but in hospital scrubs.

The woman reached out towards Bruce, extending an arm with her palm facing upwards. Hesitantly Bruce reached his hand towards hers. As they touched, a snake like tentacle slipped out of her skin. It wrapped itself tightly around his arm, all the way up to his shoulder. The tentacle glowed brightly pulling Bruce in closer to the woman. Her face became frantic as she leaned in close and her skin turned translucent. Instinctively, Bruce pulled away but she was significantly stronger. Bruce could hear intense crackling, like an electrical explosion, emanating from her.

Bruce struggled as she whispered into his ear "Help her."

He stopped struggling and looked into her eyes. Teardrops made of light fell from her face. Frozen, he stared at her, shocked. She let go of his arm and he fell backwards landing with a thump; again on his rear.

Bruce looked up as the field dissolved into his dorm room and he found himself entangled in sweat-soaked bedsheets, lying awkwardly on his floor. A soft tap emanated from the interior of his bathroom door. It swung open and Lian popped her head in, asking if everything was alright. She had heard loud noises coming from his room and was worried. Nodding sheepishly at her, Bruce held the sheet at his waist awkwardly. An embarrassed flush washed over his face as he mumbled something indistinct. Lian looked at him curiously for a moment but left without argument.

Still sitting on the floor Bruce shook his head in disbelief. Looking up Bruce saw the football jersey on the wall above his bed, Something on it seemed out of place. Jumping to his feet he trips over the sheets that he is still tangled in. He rips them away from his body and makes his way towards it. Under the signature 'HELP HER' is scrawled in big, bold letters. He blinked his eyes a few times, rubbing them. When he opened them again the words were gone. He looked around the room and then towards the bathroom that separated him from Lian. He wondered what was going to happen to her.

Lian shuffled her feet, dragging herself slowly along campus. Her last class of the day had ended a half hour ago but Bruce still had two more classes. Becoming listless Lian had began to wander aimlessly about. She found herself in one of many small gardens adorned with fancy benches and a gazebo. She sat down in the gazebo, closing her eyes as she leaned back relaxing.

"Mind if I join you?" a male voice asked her and her eyes fluttered open. She saw Darin and closed her eyes again without giving an answer. "No answer is not a no, I hope," Darin said as he sat down beside her.

They sat in silence for several minutes. At one point Lian thought she felt his fingertips grazed her hand but when she snuck a look his hands were in his lap. She sighed softly and leaned further back into the bench.

"I'm sorry, was I disturbing your solitude?"

Lian shook her head no, then laughed, realizing that Darin may have his eyes shut too. "No, not at all. Just taking a moment to enjoy the tranquility. Company is not discouraged," She said as she opened her eyes.

Darin smiled at her and opened his eyes. Lian saw that he had a roughly made bouquet, in his hand. He held them out to her, attempting to look meek about it. She could barely stop staring at his chest as she took in the tightness of his shirt and how it moved as he thrusted the flowers towards her. She accepted them, a small, pink flush blooming on her face.

"I..uh.. kinda stole them. Technically," Darin said as he indicated the flowers in the garden matched the ones she held. Lian laughed aloud and placed a hand over her mouth to muffle her laughter. "Its nice to see you laugh," He said and Lian abruptly grew quiet, her face flustered.

"I try," Lian said, embarrassed.

"So," Darin said quickly, trying to change the topic, "do you have any more classes this afternoon?"

Lian shook her head, "Nope, done for the day. Just a few mountains of homework to scale and lab assignments to work on." She stood up and stretched her legs out one by one.

"Me too," Darin said softly, flexing his fingers on his lap, "Do you suppose, I could walk you back to your dorm?"

Lian turned to look at him, her arms stretched out above her head, surprised at his inquiry. The look on her face must have made him thought she was upset because he began to apologize profusely. She leaned over, grazed his arm with her hand before grabbing his hands with hers, "I'd be honoured."

A large smile grew on Darin's face and he stood up too quickly, bumping his head into her shoulder. They both struggled to regain their balance and while she managed to keep hers, he fell over. She laughed and held a hand out to help him back up.

"I'm not normally a klutz, I swear," Darin said sheepishly as Lian laughed again. He took her arm in his and the two of them walked out of the garden chatting.

When they arrived at her building, Lian pulled her arm out of his and turned to face him. "Sorry for such a short walk."

"It was nice. I would like to do it again, if you'd like."

"That would be nice," She said with a smile.

Darin leaned in to kiss her. As their lips met she felt herself give in slightly before she resisted and pulled away. Darin began to apologize again and Lian waved it off, claiming to not be ready yet and asking for his forgiveness. Opening the door to the lobby she looked he was walking away, his shoulders hunched low. Lian went to call out to him, but couldn't quite bring herself to. She watched until he was out of sight before clutching her hands to her chest. Her face flushed she smiled and thought about how she just had her first kiss.

Lian closed her door the smile still on her face, her cheeks bright pink. She looked over her shoulder, part of her hoping he'd still be standing out where she could see him, but Darin was already gone. Lian shook her head, like an embarrassed high school girl. She passed the reception desk barely noticing the student working it, her nose buried in a textbook. Much like everyone else on campus, they were all preparing for final exams. She thought about asking for her mail, but decided against it and made her way towards the stairwell.

As she pushed the door open she heard her name and turned back to face the reception desk. The girl working the counter had set her textbook on the countertop and was waving an envelope in her hand. She looked excited so Lian rushed back over to the desk.

"You have all the luck, don't you?" the girl said her eyes lighting up. "And in your first semester."

Lian looked puzzled as the girl handed the envelope over. "Whatever are you talking about?" she asked as she perused the envelope. The metallic calligraphy lettering showed the return address to be from the HD Centre at John Hopkins Hospital.

"A job offer this early on and hand delivered by such a hunk!" The girl said, clutching her hands to her chest and sighing.

Lian gave her a small smile, shoved the envelope into her bag, and headed for the staircase.

"You're not going to open it now?" the girl called out as Lian disappeared into the stairwell.

Lian ran up the stairs, her heart lurching. She dashed down the hallway and into her room. She held herself against the door; her breathing laboured and fear in her eyes. Lian took the envelope out, letting her bag slide off her shoulder and onto the floor with a thud. She looked at the envelope briefly before rushing through the bathroom and into Bruce's room. She scanned the room silently, knowing he would still be in class, before returning to her room and sitting on the bed.

Her hands trembled as she ripped the envelope open. She pulled out a single, folded, piece of paper. Closing her eyes she slowly inhaled and exhaled. Keeping her eyes closed Lian unfolded the paper in her still shaking hands. She partially opened one eye and half squinting Lian tried to read the letter. Unable to focus clearly she opened both eyes and quickly skimmed it.

The sound of a nearby door clicking open made her jump. Lian heard Bruce come into his dorm room and call out to her. She rushed over to the bathroom and simultaneously turned on the shower while slamming the door on his side shut with her foot. Bruce called out her name again and she held her breath. Lian was shaking all over as she heard him approach the bathroom door. Carefully, she reached over and quietly locked the door. As she did, she felt the doorknob jiggled beneath her fingers and she gasped softly.

"Hey, are you going to be long? I just got back from the gym and I'm kinda gross," Bruce called out to her through the door.

Lian tried to reply, but couldn't manage much more than a squeak.

"I know you can hear me, the fan isn't on. If you don't hurry up I'll come over and roll my sweaty self all over your bed," Bruce said with a laugh.

"I — I — won't be long. Promise," Lian managed to force out, in a whisper, as she pressed her face onto the door.

"Alright."

Lian heard him walk away from the door. She let out the breath that she had been holding and slid down the door until she landed on the floor. Her legs splayed out awkwardly, she hunched herself over. Tears streamed down her face. Her sobs were silent; the paper crushed within her hands.

* * *

Later that evening Lian was sitting on her bed, her legs drawn in to her chest, staring at the bottle of pills she no longer needed to take. Bruce had repeatedly knocked on her bathroom door all evening, trying to get her to unlock it. She had lost count of the number of times Bruce had knocked on the door. Her face was tear stained and sticky, her nose runny.

Lian didn't know why she couldn't just let Bruce in or why she couldn't tell him. Bruce had gone with her to the hospital and taken her for most of her tests. He knew what she was being tested for and wouldn't be surprised. But Lian just couldn't bear to face him right now. Her insides were jumbled about, she felt confused; lost and in despair. Lian looked down at the letter now on the floor and threw her pillow at it. She cried out in rage, knowing that Bruce was likely to hear her. Unsurprisingly she heard him knock on her door moments later.

Lian slid off her bed and shuffled her way over to the door. She placed her cheek against the it, the coolness of it comforting against her still warm cheek. Tears in her eyes she closed them and placed a hand on the door. Lian mumbled an apology, too soft to be heard by Bruce, before pushing herself away from the door. Silently, she slipped on some shoes and grabbed her jacket as she ran out into the hallway and away from him.

Lian found herself in the gazebo outside her dorm again. The sun was beginning to set as she sat down on the same bench and closed her eyes.

"Fancy meeting you here again. Its been what, three hours?" Darin said. Lian immediately snapped her eyes open and sat upright, her back arched with tension. Her eyes flared with anger and annoyance. Darin backed away from her, his hands in the air. "I'm sorry, I'll leave you be," He said defensively. He put his hands in his pockets and turned away from her.

Lian reached up and grabbed the edge of his jacket. Darin looked back, but her eyes were downcast and she said nothing. They were silently locked in the moment, both afraid to move. Finally she let go of his jacket, her arms going limp at her side. Darin turned her face up towards his, finding her eyes ashen and empty. Lian looked lost and as if life was slipping out of her. She appeared hollow and broken. Darin sat down beside her, put his arm around her shoulders and Lian let him pull her close. She turned her head into his shoulder and cried.

Outside the gazebo, Bruce ran past the garden in just a t-shirt and jogging pants frantically searching for Lian. Bruce had heard her door close and let himself into her room. He wondered if she was just trying to fake him out. But instead of finding her hiding in her room he had found the letter from the clinic. He ran after her in a panic, forgetting entirely to grab his jacket or hat. The temperature was near zero. His breath was came out in white puffs, but he didn't notice.

As Bruce passed the gazebo he barely notice a couple sitting on a bench. He ran into the girl who usually worked their dormitory's reception. He asked her if she had seen Lian recently and she began to gush about the letter and the dreamy hunk that had delivered it. He grabbed her by the shoulders and asked her to slow down, unable to comprehend what she was babbling about. She pointed a finger towards the gazebo.

"Him. He's the dreamboat." She sighed.

Bruce saw that she was pointing towards the couple. As Bruce got closer to them, he realized that it was Lian and Darin in a cozy embrace. Bruce clenched his fists at his sides and gritted his teeth as he turned on his heels. Just outside the gazebo he punched a tree before stalking away from the happy couple.

Chapter 6

Lian yawned as she skipped down the steps of the dorm. She had let out it all out; crying on Darin's shoulder. The two of them had chatted until the sun rose the next morning. She couldn't recall much about their conversation, just that it had felt natural and it had put her at ease. It was nice to have someone she could talk to that wasn't Bruce. She paused mid step, a twinge of guilt crossing her briefly at the thought, but she quickly shook it away. It was high time that the two of them got their independence. If she could make other friends and show that she was strong enough on her own, then Bruce might be willing to move on too. The sooner he did, the better and easier it would be for him.

Lian made her way onto campus, a small skip in her step. As she walked past the gazebo she paused slightly; a smile dancing on her lips. She continued on towards the little cafe hut that was just around the corner. She hoped that it was late enough in the morning that there wouldn't be a large lineup. Lian pulled out her phone and saw that it was twenty past ten. Most morning classes would have started, so she should fine. She had just enough time to grab a latte before her late morning lab at eleven.

As Lian rounded the bend she saw that it was indeed, her lucky morning. There was no one in line outside the hut and the open sign was still out. She did notice a relatively large group nearing the cafe so she picked up her pace, ready to cut in front of them if need be. She made it to the counter and had ordered her drink before the group managed to filter in behind her. Lian stepped to the right and waited as she munched on a freshly warmed croissant. As the barista handed her a latte she realized the sugar was on the other side of the counter through the group of chattering girls.

Lian excused herself as she tried to pass through the group. Instead of a line, they were in a large clump; rotating as they ordered. The first couple of girls let her pass by easily, but the third girl, a cheery petite blonde that was in most of her classes cut her off.

"Excuse me, but are you trying to cut the line?" the blonde said loudly, sneering.

"Uh, no? I've already got my drink," Lian said holding her cup up in defence.

"Then what are you doing?"

"Trying to get to the sugar counter. The one you're blocking," Lian said, a bit more attitude than usual in her voice.

The blonde stiffened up, her eyes flaring. One of the other girls grabbed a handful of sugar and passed them to the blonde. The blonde proceeded to rip open the sugars and pour them into Lian's cup. "Oh these sugars? You do look like you could use a few extra calories" She said haughtily, pouring packet after packet into Lian's cup. Lian just watched in shock as the blonde emptied the entire handful into her cup. "Is that sweet enough for you?" she asked rhetorically and the group of girls laughed nervously with her.

Lian held herself back from splashing the contents of her latte in the blonde's face, but only because she knew it was hot and could burn her. She'd hate to have to do first aid on the same person she had just injured. She was sure there were rules about that. Instead, she poured her latte down the front of the blonde's jacket. The girl shrieked, more in surprise than in pain and Lian took that moment to free herself from the clump of girls. She broke off in a dash and ran the whole way to her next class.

Bruce was sitting on his bedroom floor playing with his Xbox. He was trying to distract himself from the enigma that had become Lian, but the only thing he was successfully doing was ruining his stats. He looked over his shoulder towards the bathroom. The door to her room was still closed but he could see light leaking out from underneath the door. Bruce had heard Lian come home shortly after he did, but before he could get into the bathroom she had locked the door from her side. After a few futile attempts at trying to get her attention Bruce had finally given up. However, he left his door open waiting for an opportunity to catch her.

The last few days had been hell. Lian had moved away from him in class, opting to sit alone. The girls in his class saw this as an opportunity to move in like the vultures that they were. The more Bruce tried to reach out to Lian the further away she got and the more it drove the vultures in. Her bathroom door had remained locked for the most part. The odd time Bruce found it open he would see that Lian was not there. More and more he had seen her in the company of Darin and his heart continued to break. His worry was replaced with jealousy. The jealously was replaced with despair.

Shortly after getting home Bruce felt hunger pangs and ordered enough Chinese food to feed a small army. He had hoped to win her back through her stomach. Or at the very least, make sure that she was still eating. Though Lian already had a petite frame to begin with, she looked like she had lost a lot of weight. So much so that she looked gaunt whenever he could get a close enough look at her.

Bruce turned back to his game only to realize that his character was lying dead across a jeep. His buddies were crying in his ear. He sighed, offered a weak apology to the group, and signed himself out. He wouldn't be any help to them in this condition. As he shut off his television there was a knock on his door. He smiled, jumping to his feet and raced for the door. Opening it he saw the delivery man and Bruce slapped a few bills into his free hand. Bruce took the multiple bags of food to his desk and rearranged the food to fill one of the bags to the brim. He shoved on a baseball cap, grabbed the bag, and walked over to Lian's front door.

With the bag of food held up high enough to hide most of his face Bruce knocked on the door and shouted, "Delivery," in a fake Swedish accent. He heard the scuffle of feet as she came to the door to investigate. He held the bag up and waved it in front of his face.

"I didn't order any delivery, you have the wrong room."

"Uhh, special order, paid for you by a friend," Bruce mumbled, trying to maintain his fake Swedish accent.

He heard the sound of the latch being removed and eagerly took a step forward. He heard the latch quickly being redone.

"Nice try Bruce. Just leave me alone please." He heard Lian move away from the door and further into her room.

"Lian," Bruce called out to her, "Please. We need to talk. About what happened the other week."

"Go away," Lian shouted. She held her hand up in front of face and turned it over slowly. She closed her eyes and concentrated as hard as she could. Her hand sparked slightly, but Lian couldn't reproduce what had happened the other day. Whenever she had tried her heart had grown heavy with sadness and she didn't understand why.

Bruce lowered the bag and put a hand on her door. "I know you're sick. I saw the letter," He said softly. He gave the door one last longing look before admitting defeat and headed back to his own room. He put the bag of Chinese food on his desk. His appetite may be gone but his determination wasn't. Bruce went back into the bathroom and searched through the cabinets. After a few minutes he found Lian's tool box. He emptied the contents on the floor, in front of her locked door, and began to take apart the doorknob.

After several minutes Bruce had managed to remove the screws and was gently pulling his side of the doorknob off. He didn't want her side to fall off but instead wanted to pull the latch from the inside mechanism and unlock it. As he set the knob down into his lap he listened carefully to see if Lian had heard him. Bruce contemplated knocking on the bathroom door, to judge where Lian was in the room but didn't want the knob to fall off on her side and lock them both out of the bathroom.

Bruce inserted a screwdriver in the centre part of the inner guts and pushed the latch, with much difficulty, out of the doorframe. The door quietly swung open. He quickly got to his feet, dropping the tools and hardware all over the floor. He called out her name as he burst into her room, only to find her room empty. The window above her bed was open, the curtains fluttering. He leaned out the window and saw that Lian had attached a rope from her bed frame that reached down to the ground below. Bruce shook his head as he pulled the rope up and coiled it neatly. He place it on her bed and went back to his room, leaving the tool box and hardware scattered on the bathroom floor.

Lian stood in the middle of an open field that stretched out for miles. The sun was high above her. In the far off distance tiny little trees dotted the edge of a nearby village. Beyond it were mountains that stretched out encapsulating the forest, the village and the very field that she stood in. The grass was quite high, well past her knees, and it was adorned with large dandelions ready to seed, daisies and random patches of sunflowers. The flowers towered over her fairly short height.

At the moment, however, Lian felt remarkably tall. She had no proof, nothing solid to compare her height too, just a feeling. There were other things that felt different as well. She could see that her hair was much longer than normal and had a reddish tinge to it. Overall, Lian felt stronger and her body more toned. As Lian looked around the field she felt an overwhelming sense of déjà vu mixed with dread. Inside something was screaming at her; telling her to leave. It told her to run away as quickly as possible, but a stronger force compelled to go to the village. Something was going to happen soon. It was something she either had to see or be a part of.

As Lian strode across the field, purpose filling her veins she found herself moving at a pace much faster than one normally could. She felt as if Hermes wings were on her feet and she laughed. The village quickly grew bigger as Lian filled the gap between her and it. A quick glance over her shoulder revealed that the forest was now engulfed in flames. Lian blinked rapidly. The flames disappeared and then reappeared. It was as if both states existed in the same moment. Lian tried to turn around so she could take a better look at the forest, but her feet were moving of their own accord. Turning back to the village Lian saw it was only a few feet away and shrouded in darkness. Stopping at the village edge, she cautiously peered in. It was mid afternoon. The sun shone brightly in the field where she stood. The village, however, was pitch black, as if in nighttime. A line stood at her feet where the sunlight and the moonlight met. A quick look behind her revealed the whole field completely engulfed in flames, as if mocking her, should she try to avoid the village.

It was then that Lian noticed a giant scythe in her hand. It towered a few feet above her in height. The blade as long as she was tall. She noticed that she was wearing a flowing and very see through white gown with short sleeves and a long hood. Her skin had taken on a translucent pale blue look. None of these changes surprised her, but her heart filled with dread as she stepped across the threshold into the dark village.

Lian walked through the darkness as if she had done this before. She knew, instinctively, that not only was this her first time there, but that it would also be her last.

Weaving through the tiny huts Lian made her way towards the town's centre. There she found a large water fountain adorned with an elegant statue of a man, probably the village founder, in the middle. Surrounding the fountain was a large open space. It was filled with many villagers enjoying the splendours of a crisp and calm evening. The villagers seemed blissfully unaware of the fires that raged just outside their village. Nimbly, Lian leapt from the ground to the edge of the fountain and then to atop of the statue. She barely had the time to register that she had accomplished this feat before Lian realized that she was lifting the scythe high above her head. She closed her eyes and mumbled some words in a language that she didn't recognize, but knew weren't foreign to her. She could feel her heart racing with fear, confusion, resentment, anger, and pity. It was as if there was another being inside guiding her through the motions. Lian couldn't tell if she was dreaming, reliving the past, or experiencing it for the first time.

With her eyes still closed Lian felt a breeze wrap itself around her body; from the bottom of her feet, all the way up to the tip of her fingers and over to the scythe. It was as if the breeze was coming from her itself. She felt it growing rapidly and then quickly disperse outwards from her scythe. Lian opened her eyes and saw several small dots of light begin to appear above the tiny huts throughout the village. At first there were only a couple that shined big and bright, but then more began to appear. Her eyes filled with tears as within mere seconds almost the entire village lit up with these mysterious little lights and screams.

Chapter 7

Lian's eyes flew wide open and she found herself in complete darkness. Lian bolted upright into a seated position and frantically looked from side to side, but the village was long gone. There was no more fire, no more fountain, no more little lights. There were no more screams except for the ones inside her head. She was back in her dorm room, the horror of her nightmare slowly withdrawing.

Lian fumbled for the cup of water that she kept next to her bed. Her hands trembled violently, accidentally knocking the cup off the nightstand. Water splashed everywhere but the cup, thankfully, was plastic. It bounced harmlessly onto the hardwood floor and rolled under her desk.

Pulling her knees into her chest Lian cried. The nightmare lingered far longer than any dream had before. She couldn't get their screams out of her head. She didn't understand what was happening with the lights that she had seen, but Lian knew that she had done something terrible. Their screams reminded her of the screams from horror movies, when people were being violently killed off. They were the terrifying shrieks of pain of those dying mixed the with horrible cries of those watching loved ones die.

Lian didn't understand what it meant or why had she done what she did. She didn't understand why the other presence inside of her felt so familiar. Turning on her bedside lamp Lian got out of bed, retrieved her cup from under the desk, and went into the bathroom to refill it. As Lian drank the water something caught her attention out of the corner of her eye. The moonlight was reflecting off of her hair into the mirror. She turned on the bathroom lights and discovered that a very small patch of her hair had turned bright red. Leaning further in, to better examine it, she held it out like it was a foreign object. Lian moaned softy as she ripped the red strands of hair out and flushed them down the toilet.

Still crying, Lian ran back into her room, slipped on the water and fell onto her bed. Her chest heaving up and down heavily as she choked back the sobs. Was she still dreaming? What did any of this mean? Propping herself up onto her elbows Lian looked towards the bathroom light. Bruce's door was ajar and Lian could hear him snoring in his bed. Without much thought she grabbed her pillow, blanket and journal then marched into Bruce's room, turning off the light as she walked through the bathroom. Lian grabbed the two cushions off of the love seat in his room and laid them on the floor next to his bed; much like they did when they were children, having sleepovers. She put her pillow on the edge of the cushions, lay down on them, and covered herself with the blanket. The screams in her head finally quieted down. A smile arose on her lips as she snuggled up inside her blankets and quickly fell asleep.

The sun blasted through the partially opened curtains in his room. Bruce pulled the blankets up over his head and grumbled. A single arm popped out from beneath the covers and flailed about trying to close the curtains from the offending sunlight impeding on his sleep. He only succeeded in pulling his covers further off. With another grumble Bruce sat up and glared out at the sun cresting over the mountains. His hair was flattened on the one side and his cheek indented with the criss cross pattern of his pillowcases' embroidery. He grabbed the curtain, pulled it shut, and flopped back onto his bed.

As Bruce was pulling the blankets back up, a small movement caught his eye. He groaned, now fully awake he admitted defeat on getting back to sleep. Bruce pushed the covers back and got out of bed. He felt his foot connect with a pillow on the ground. Bruce grunted as he stood up, kicking the pillow out of his way. It landed softly a few inches away from Lian who mumbled in her sleep as she rolled over to her other side. Bruce nudged Lian gently with one foot. She sighed in her sleep and curled up even further into a ball. He sat back down and rolled over to the window. Bruce cracked the curtain open a bit and saw that Lian was indeed, lying on his floor.

Bruce knelt down, put a hand on her forehead and felt for a temperature. Nestled beside her makeshift bed was her dream journal. The one he suggested she start years ago when they were kids, to help her keep track of her nightmares. When they were younger Lian often had terrible nightmares. Whenever she did she would crawl out her bedroom window to the treehouse that adjoined their properties to write in her dream journal. She would then crawl over through his window and curl up onto his lower bunk. It was an old elementary school notebook, tattered and torn, with its edges frayed by age. Barely able to hold itself together.

Bruce gently stroked her cheek, fondly remembering the treehouse that connected their bedrooms. He grabbed the dream journal and slid his arms under her shoulders and knees, pulling her up off of the floor. It was an easy scoop, as

Lian had lost so much weight recently. Quietly, Bruce made his way to her room, set Lian in her own bed without waking her up and wrapped her in several blankets. Bruce set the dream journal under Lian's pillow and sat down on the bed beside her. He kissed Lian gently on the forehead and she smiled in her sleep.

"Oh Lian, why are you doing this to yourself? Why are pushing me away?" Bruce said softly before getting up and going back to his own bed.

Lian rushed into the classroom, mere moments before class started. The professor was already seated in the front row. Lian's hair was haphazardly pulled into a large clip with random bits sticking out and her cheeks still had the pillow indentations on her face. Her blouse was buttoned up incorrectly and although not seen, Lian wore two different socks. She dashed to the lectern, pulling a file folder stuffed full of notes she had jammed into it first thing that morning. Pieces of paper trickled out as she opened the folder on the lectern. She pulled out a set of recipe cards that she had marked up as cue cards. They went flying out of her hands like a game of 52 pickup.

Lian's classmates, who were milling about and settling in their seats, snickered. Lian sighed as she knelt down, gathering her cards. She could hear the nearest group of girls laughing and muttering to themselves about her incompetency. Bruce chose that exact moment to stroll in, ignore the snickering girls and turn to the lectern to see Lian crawling on the ground gathering the cue cards. Without a word, Bruce knelt down beside Lian, gathered her cards, put them on the lectern and took his seat.

Lian stood up and began to shuffle through the papers in preparation of her oral report. Her paper was on the theory of the evolution of medicine throughout religious practice.

Despite being an easy pass class, most students took it because it didn't have a final exam. The report she was about to give made up for 70% of her grade. She was guaranteed a pass just for giving it, regardless of how accurate the content may or may not be. Which meant, in most cases, students just made a half ass attempt at their report and no one paid any real attention when they presented.

Lian hadn't slept well the night before, having fallen asleep on Bruce's floor yet again. Nor had she slept well in days. She was having the same reoccurring nightmares, like they were a broken record stuck on repeat. They had become so intense as of late, that she now kept her dream journal under her pillow. The dreams tore and ripped at her in ways she had never known possible. Fear clung greedily to her for hours afterwards. Even when she couldn't recall a single detail. She could re-read her journal to her hearts content but the words she wrote were nothing more than that — meaningless words. As the days dragged on she re-read the entries multiple times. They began to linger in her mind. They nagged at her; tugged at her. Pulled her down so far into the pits of despair that she found herself unable to cope with much. She dragged herself about from class to class like a mindless drone.

Bruce, Lian thought, had yet to take notice of the bags under her eyes and she continued to push him away to the point where she felt it would be wrong to call him back. She couldn't play with his heart that way. Despite that, Lian kept finding herself in his room curled up on the pillows at the base of his bed, much like when they were kids. She had, for the most part, always managed to sneak back to her room unnoticed. But she knew she couldn't keep going on like this.

The clock chimed on the hour and the students quickly took their seats. Unlike a lot of other classes the students enjoyed this one immensely. The reports, regardless of how dry the topic might be, had only one mandatory obligation to them. All reports must be accompanied with a visual presentation. The definition of these parameters were left to the imagination of the individual student. Last week a student had created a animated video with Play-Doh, G.I. Joes, and my little ponies. The conversations in the video were dubbed, quite likely by his younger siblings as he narrated the entire video as if it were a documentary.

Lian had created a slide show on her computer using fancy templates for picture transitions. The professor turned off the lights and took his seat in the front row, an unopened notebook in his lap. She adjusted the light on the lectern over her notes and started the slideshow. She had underscored it with light music in hopes to avoid any awkward silences that she knew would probably occur. She hated giving oral reports almost as much as she hated the nightmares.

The first picture that popped up was that of the milky way galaxy. She stared at it dumbly, confused as it was supposed to be one of the medical symbol of a cross covered in snakes. She looked at at her laptop and could see the image she wanted and not the milky way one that was up on the screen. She confirmed that her laptop was connected to the projector and looked at it in confusion as she tried to pick up the remote. Her hands were shaking so badly that it jumped about and fell onto the floor. A few students giggled as she squatted down, looking for it. She felt around for it, but couldn't find anything beneath the desk. Looking back at the screen she saw scripture weaving itself onto the screen. It read "The Universe: Conceptions, Reality and Existence". The milky way dissipated and was replaced with a orange glowing orb. It was pulsing a vibrant orange and yellow, as if it were living and breathing. A golden cage dissolved over top of it and a man, dressed in all white, appeared outside the cage. The sound of a heartbeat could be heard softly in the background. The beating of the heartbeat matched that pulse of the glowing orb.

She gasped softly. She knew this orb. Instinctively she knew what it was and its importance. A switch went off inside her head. She slowly stood back up and turned to face her classmates with a sad smile on her face.

"This world is much more interconnected than you could ever imagine. There is more life than you will ever dream of and we are all dependent on each other in ways you can barely comprehend," she started, her voice a mere whisper, as if she were telling a ghost story at a campfire. The screen behind her grew dark as the pulsing orb slowly faded out, as if dying.

Everyone grew quiet. Pencils were set down, earbuds were removed and phones were put into bags. The whole classroom suddenly shifted their focused onto her and her hypnotic voice. It was like she had transformed into an entirely different person right before their eyes. Lian's eyes sparkled and her face danced within the shadows cast by the projector. Her voice pulled you in and held you tight.

"Imagine that the universe is self sustaining. That there are species whose primary function is to create various life forms. No single race has the power to do everything, but they all equally contribute in the creation of a sustainable ecosystem and the life within it. It is all separated into various tasks. One species creates the planets; one creates the moons and; another creates the stars. Then there are species that create plant life, lakes, rocks, and mountains. Another creates less intelligent animal life and lastly, only the most evolved beings of all, the one that created the existence of the entire universe itself, can create intelligent life," Lian said softly. She looked out at her classmates and saw that they were hanging on her every word. Smiling, Lian pressed forward.

She told them how everything had a soul — absolutely

everything, including plants, trees, animals, lakes, and beings. She explained that every soul was created equal to another and that every soul lived as many different lives as was possible. Lian explained that you could be a tree for one lifetime and a water mammal the next. You could spend your entire life on one side of the universe or live each of your corporal body's life in a different section of the universe. You could flit from one planet to another. Things took time to create, so life was essentially ever growing. In higher forms of intelligent life, it wasn't uncommon to develop a fondness for a specific tree or type of plant life. Usually one similar to one you had been in a previous incarnation. You remembered your past like a warmth that wrapped your heart. Déjà vu was a norm in life. That each soul had an overall life expectancy. When it lived its last life and died, it would fall into a limbo like sleep.

It was a fairly simple system when you thought about it. A large, gigantic empty vast space of nothingness was the template you began with. Then in the centre you start small but steady; like the tortoise that won the race against the hare. You lay in your foundation. Only the basics are needed like your commanders in charge and some simple supplies. Then slowly you build from there. When you reached a good point you break off some of your people and expand further and further out. Then you just keep growing and growing; just living and experiencing like a newly married couple. First they buy a condo just for the two of them. Then they have a child and move into a bigger condo. Then another child and a dog comes along and they buy a small house. Then her mother in law falls ill so they buy a bigger house. And so on, and so on.

Then, when the universe itself had grown as much as it could and for as long as it could, it too died. And everything with it. Until nothing was left but the empty vast nothingness. Then it started all over again.

The screen behind her had filled with vivid images of planets, solar systems, exploding stars, black holes, comets, falling stars, and finally various alien species. Every alien ever seen on television or film flashed before their faces. It happened slowly at first, then more and more rapidly like someone hit a fast forward button. They were interspersed with shots of outer space and its never ending content. As Lian finished the screen fell into darkness. In the far distance, a small, orange glow of light flickered softly. She looked at it fondly, with a soft but sad smile on her face, cloudiness flickering briefly in her eyes.

The whole classroom was dead silent, their breaths drew in like a gasp they were unable to let go of. Then the lights suddenly snapped on and after a moment of deafening silence the entire class broke out in thunderous applause. They shouted and cheered and screamed. It was as if they were at a concert and the main band had just walked onto the stage. Several students stood up and whistled loudly.

Lian smiled awkwardly, her eyes blinking. She held out her arms in front, waving them downwards, urging the students to quiet down. Hesitantly they took their seats again and grew quiet, eager to hear what else she would have to say. She glanced briefly at Bruce, who was staring at her dumbly. She knew what he was thinking, the two of them originally had similar ideas for their reports so initially they had researched together and split the details that they found so their reports would differ and also support each other. Looking at the glowing orange orb on the screen she wondered what had just happened. She was afraid that this fountain of knowledge would suddenly evaporate from her mind. Lian could feel her heart beating wildly.

She turned back to her classmates and smiled briefly. "Are there any questions?" she asked as every hand, Bruce's included, shot into the air. Lian ignored him and pointed to a girl seated at the far back of the classroom. As the girl asked her question Lian saw her phone light up with a message from Bruce. She ignored it, but he continued to send it again and again. Finally, she snuck a quick look at the pictures Bruce sent. One was a close up of her hands and the other her eyes. Lian looked down in horror to see her a soft blue light emanating from her hands. She placed them on the lectern out of sight of her classmates. The picture of her eyes showed that her normal dull hazel colour was now a vibrant, glittering green. Lian looked at Bruce with shock and surprise. Their eyes met for a moment and he could see the green colour fading from her eyes, like water pouring down a wall. For a brief second they flickered and then flared a bright green right before she fainted.

Lian was still sitting at the professor's desk, an ice pack on her head, as the class finished. The students had lingered briefly, hoping to talk to her, but then dispersed when it looked like she wasn't able to handle the attention. Bruce had lingered longer than the rest, insisting that he take her to the nurse's office. She waved him off, telling him to not miss his next class. Despite all attempts of persuasion from Bruce, Lian pushed him away. Disappointed, Bruce left her alone with the professor and trotted off.

The professor had talked her through the steps of a concussion test multiple times and was satisfied that she was okay. She had feigned a lack of appetite and poor eating mixed with nerves on doing the oral presentation as her reason for fainting. When Lian had finally convinced him that she was fine he let her gather her things and leave.

Outside of the classroom Lian leaned up against the wall and sighed heavily. She didn't notice Bruce hovering just down the hallway, waiting anxiously for her. She gingerly put a hand to her head and touched the back of it carefully. It was quite tender from where she had hit it. Thankfully, when Lian had fainted she did the 'traditional' faint and not the 'movie' faint. Her whole body crumpled into itself and she fell straight down, only hitting her head from a fall of about a foot off the ground. Lian closed her eyes and willed the pain away.

"I heard you took quite the tumble," Darin said, mysteriously appearing beside her.

Lian opened her eyes briefly and then shut them again, not wanting to stare obviously. Darin was once again wearing an incredibly tight shirt half unbuttoned. "Word travels fast."

"We are barely out of high school, aren't we?" Darin said with a smile.

"Hmmhmm."

"I heard you gave quite the presentation. Not sure you needed the sympathy vote from your professor though."

Lian burst out laughing, "No, I guess not."

"Can I buy you a coffee?" Darin asked as he held out his jacket and revealed a flask hidden within it. "I'll even sweeten the deal and help you with your headache." He held out his arm towards her.

Lian took his arm and smiled back, "That sounds marvellous."

The two of them walked down the hallway towards one of the many little cafe kiosks set up on campus. Neither of them saw Bruce just a bit further down the hallway, his teeth clenched, seething with hatred and his eyes filled with wild jealousy. As the two of them exited the building he kicked the wall nearest him with fury.

Despite being fairly large in size, the grocery store maintained a small and quaint atmosphere. Lian opted for a basket despite her potentially large list. She was debating on whether or not she should stock up for the winter. She had split the cost of a small freezer and a couple of hot plates with Bruce as she wasn't sure what winters here would be like and was used to having a freezer full of easy to heat up snacks and meals. The freezer sat in the hallway outside their rooms and they each had a single hot plate. Most of the time both of the hot plates were in her room, making it easier to prepare a proper meal, but with the given circumstances, she had shucked one of them back into Bruce's room, hoping he would take the hint.

Lian's phone chirped and she grimaced slightly when she saw it was Bruce. She had waited until Bruce had gone to practice before heading out to shop. Apparently it was over early and he had borrowed the teams van having the same idea as her. She closed her phone and put it on silent, knowing it was unlikely he'd come to this exact store since she had also intentionally gone out of town to a new store neither of them had gone to before.

Impulsively, Lian decided on hiring a taxi to take her home so she swapped her basket for a cart before making her way down the baking aisle. She filled the cart with flour, sugar, chocolate, and a variety of cake mixes. Lian preferred to make things from scratch, but the boxed cake mix always tasted better when she made them in the slow cooker. Lian was debating what kind of chocolate chips to get for the cookies when a set of arms wrapped around her waist and hoisted her high into the air. Lian shrieked as Bruce tried to put her into the cart with the food. He had half succeeded despite her kicking and punching. Bruce's laughter cut out abruptly when he saw that Lian wasn't laughing with him, nor laughing at all.

"What the hell are you doing here?" Lian asked, her voice an angry growl as she still struggled in his arms.

"The guys wanted a lift nearby and I passed this store on

the way. Thought I'd might as well stop here. Why does it matter?" Bruce said sheepishly.

"Never mind, just put me down and go."

Bruce set her down on the ground beside him, her body gliding gently against his. Lian felt her body's urge to gasp involuntarily, but bit her tongue to stop herself. As a small shudder did escape she turned away from Bruce, her face flushed. Bruce thankfully misinterpreted her reactions and took a step back, obviously hurt.

"Whats going on with you?" Bruce asked, his voice wavering. "You keep acting all high and mighty in person, but then you practically crawl into bed with me each night."

Lian's face scrunched up, fighting back the tears, keeping her back to him. "Nothing, alright? There is nothing going on between us so stop acting like there is." She spat out.

Lian turned to see his face crumpled and his heart shattering at her words. She forced herself to stand her ground as she grabbed her cart and marched off down the aisle.

As Lian disappeared from sight Bruce cast aside his dignity and chased after her. He wasn't going to lose her without a fight; he would not lose her that easily. Actions spoke louder than words and everything Lian did was subconsciously calling out to him. He popped out of the end of the aisle and looked from side to side. He continued down the main row looking down each aisle until he finally found her. As Bruce made his way towards Lian he realized that she was talking to Darin. Bruce felt his skin crawl as he gritted his teeth together tightly. Lian looked up and saw Bruce approaching. She pushed her cart towards Darin and let Darin put an arm around her shoulders. As Bruce reached out to grab Lian another girl from campus put a hand on his shoulder.

"Bruce, right?" she asked, a bright smile on her face. Bruce mumbled a vague reply but she ignored his disinterest. "Do you think you could teach me how to make those Canadian butter tarts? I've heard so many good things about them."

Bruce looked at her and felt his wall crumble beneath her brilliant smile. He looked back to find Lian but realized that she and Darin had taken that opportunity to disappear. Bruce felt his heart sink as he turned back to face the young woman behind him.

"Sure. Lets go see if this country has corn syrup first," Bruce said softly as she took his arm and they wandered off towards the baking aisle.

Lian burst out of the store with Darin hot on her heels. She made it across the parking lot before collapsing on a picnic bench. She fell into a heap, crying. Hesitantly, Darin sat down beside her unsure of what to do. After a few moments, when it appeared she wasn't going to stop crying, he placed a hand on her head and and started stroking her hair softly. Her tears began to subside and she sat up, facing the parking lot and began to wipe the tears from her face. Lian looked at Darin and smiled weakly. She leaned in towards him and he pulled her into a hug.

At the same moment, a dejected Bruce walked out of the grocery store towards the van parked closest to the picnic bench. Noticing them a low growl involuntarily emitted out of his throat. Darin smiled smugly as Bruce unloaded his groceries into the van before slamming the door shut. Lian jumped slightly and looked up. She saw Bruce glaring at them and instinctively pushed herself away slightly from Darin, but he held her tight and she didn't resist.

Her whole body was suddenly wracked with pain. Lian felt her heart lurch inside, echoing loudly throughout her whole body. Her head started to shake violently from side to side and everything around her swayed slowly at first, and then more quickly. It was like a roller coaster ride that had just hit its first crescendo.

Rebecca Jayne Heipel

Darin, confused and startled, quickly let go of her. Lian reached a hand out to steady herself and found nothing but air in front of her.

Bruce was about to get into the van when he heard Darin gasp loudly. Bruce turned to see what was causing his commotion and saw Lian convulsing on the bench. Bruce watched helplessly as Lian crumpled down towards the ground. He hopped out of the van and dashed over to her, catching before she could hit the ground. Her face was scrunched up in pain as she shook violently. Bruce took one of her hands and tried soothing her. Lian wasn't epileptic nor was she having a typical seizure, but Bruce hadn't seen her have one of these attacks since they were little kids. Bruce held her tight and told Darin, now cowering on the other side of the picnic table, to call for an ambulance.

Chapter 8

Bruce was pacing the waiting room of the hospital. He was just as upset at Darin for not coming as he was worried about Lian. How long had her symptoms been back? How much had Lian been hiding from him and for how long? When they had gotten to the hospital Bruce had been escorted to the side to fill out multiple forms. He had needed to answer questions about her medical history so they could pull up her information while the doctors tended to her more immediate needs. Much to Bruce's surprise when they found her medical records sent via her family doctor back he had been informed that he was Lian's medical legal guardian. Her parents had assigned him this responsibility years ago but never told him.

His heart had deflated when they read this information to him. Bruce knew that Lian's relationship with her parents had always been strained, given she had developed her illness shortly after being adopted. It had grown significantly worse after they had their first biological child. Despite all of that, Lian had always studied hard, participated in several after school activities, and had graduated from high school as valedictorian. Yet Lian's accomplishments never seemed to be enough for her parents to care.

The doctor came to Bruce with more questions than updates. Three hours had past since the last time Bruce had seen the doctor. The doctor had hinted that he felt Lian may have a chronic illness but didn't press Bruce for more information. Bruce wondered if he should tell the doctor about the form he had found in Lian's room, confirming that she did indeed have a chronic illness, Huntington's. But every time Bruce went to bring it up the doctor had peppered him with more questions. Although Bruce was certain that Lian's current symptoms had nothing to do with Huntington's and telling the doctor would only confuse him more. Bruce sat down in a chair, put his head in his hands and sighed heavily.

"Bruce? Bruce Aldwin?" a nurse called out.

Instinctively Bruce held his hand up, forgetting that he wasn't back in school. He got up and walked over towards the nurse. She held open a door and Bruce walked through it, following her down a series of hallways until they came upon a row of curtained rooms. The majority of them were empty but recently used. Lian was in the middle of the row. The nurse pointed to a row of chairs across from the curtain and indicated that Bruce should sit down and wait for the doctor to return.

Bruce nestled into the chair and leaned back, trying to get comfortable. At least, Bruce thought to himself, these chairs were a bit comfier than the ones in the other waiting room. Bruce wasn't sure how much time had passed but he awoke to the doctor gently shaking his shoulder.

"Bruce?" the doctor said softly, rousing him out of sleep.

Bruce rubbed his eyes and wiped the drool off of his chin. He stood up, stumbling a bit, but the doctor eased Bruce back into his seat and sat down beside Bruce.

"It's best we let her rest as much as she can," the doctor

said.

When Bruce looked in the direction of where Lian was sleeping, he noticed that the other curtains were all drawn back and the beds redone neatly.

"She has Huntington's," Bruce blurted out suddenly.

The doctor gave a sad chuckle, "I had my suspicions. It took a little digging, but I managed to find her test results from the John Hopkins Centre. As luck would have it we are closely associated with their studies."

"Do you think, this was caused by that?" Bruce asked, already knowing the answer, but hoping desperately for a quick fix of some kind.

The doctor shook his head, "Unfortunately no, I don't think so. From what you told me these symptoms used to occur frequently when she was a child but then cleared up a few years ago correct?" Bruce nodded in agreement. The doctor looked at his charts and then back at Bruce before clearing his throat. "I'll be honest with you. I have no idea what could be causing her symptoms. We've run a series of tests and so far everything has come back negative."

Bruce sighed heavily and the doctor put a hand on his shoulder.

"We will figure this out. This is one of the best hospitals in Europe and it has an incredibly diligent research facility. She'll have to spend the night and we will do more intensive and probably invasive tests tomorrow morning before she can leave. But you should rest too. You're welcome to spend the night here, but I'd recommend going home. These chairs are not as comfortable as they first appear," the doctor said with a sad faraway look on his face. He stood up and shook Bruce's hand before disappearing down the hallway.

Bruce snuck a quick peek at Lian to confirm that she was indeed sleeping. Quietly and carefully he picked up the chair he had just been sitting in and dragged it into her curtained off room. He sat back down in it and settled in for a long night.

Lian lay in the hospital bed, the privacy curtain pulled around with only a small sliver of open space to peek through. She awoke on her back with an IV in her arm and a nurse taking her vitals. Bruce was sitting on the other side of the bed, her free hand in his. The IV machine beeped and the nurse quickly switched the bags over and reset the device. She took the thermometer out of Lian's mouth, wrote in the chart and disappeared. She turned to face Bruce for the first time since she had collapsed and smiled weakly. She motioned to talk but he put a finger on her lips and urged her to keep her strength, telling her to let bygones be bygones. He ran a hand along her head, patting down her wayward hair and smiled. He stood up, kissed her on the forehead and let go of her hand. She clutched his hand quickly, fear flickering across her eyes.

Bruce squeezed her hand back tightly. "I'm not leaving, I just gotta go, you know," Lian sighed with relief. "Want a juice?" he asked. She nodded eagerly in return as he left the curtained area.

Looking back he could see how tiny and weak she looked. His eyes clouded over briefly and he shook his head to clear it. Bruce wandered the many hallways until he found an open cafeteria. He purchased apple and orange juice boxes plus a brownie before wandering off in search of a restroom.

He put his food items on the bathroom counter before stepping in front of the urinal. As he stood there he let his mind wander. Bruce wasn't sure what to do with her. How long would Lian let him back in? Was coming with her to this school the wrong choice? He shook his head, trying to clear his thoughts and doubts from his mind.

"She's getting worse, isn't she?" a man said suddenly and

Bruce jumped, almost spraying the side of the urinal. It was the same man from his dream.

Bruce finished, zipped up his pants and closed his eyes. "This is just a dream. Just a terrible dream. You're not real," he mumbled to himself before opening his eyes to not only see the man still standing there, but that he had been joined by the woman. "Christ," Bruce muttered under his breath as he pushed his way through them both heading towards the sink to wash his hands. He turned on the tap and began to wash his hands. He stopped and looked back at them curiously. Leaving the water running Bruce turned back towards them and walked through them again. Literally and physically through them like they were ghosts. He waved his hands thru them several times before returning to the sink. Shocked, he finished washing his hands and wiped them on his pants. He slowly turned to face them. "What? How? Why?"

The man looked up at the woman and then at Bruce. "We're really going to loose her, aren't we dear?" he said to the woman who nodded in agreement as they both stared wistfully at Bruce.

"You're not real. Neither of you are real," Bruce stated, looking through the bathroom to see if anyone was hiding in a stall, pulling some kind of prank. "If this is a joke it isn't funny."

The woman stepped towards Bruce, reaching a hand up as if to stroke his cheek. "She needs you."

"She doesn't want me or my help," Bruce said frustrated. Trying to turn away from the woman, only to turn face first into the man. He sighed and muttered under his breath.

"Please," the woman pleaded, "She doesn't know what she needs. She's lost."

Bruce look at her, bewildered, "I don't know who you are, nor what you expect me to do. Hell, you're not even real. I mean, I can walk right through you and we all know that ghosts don't exist."

The man and woman looked at each other, their eyes full of concern.

"We're her parents," The man said softly.

Bruce blinked. He went to speak but the woman held a finger to his lips. "She's adopted and always has been. She's never born to anyone and never will be. Not even, technically, to us. We were but a vessel to bring her existence into being."

"And this is all going to end if she doesn't wake up," The man said with urgency in his voice.

"She's awake. She's just down the hall in a bed, getting medication so she'll get better, but she's awake. Come with me if you don't believe me." Upset, Bruce stormed out of the bathroom.

When he got a few feet down the hall he looked back and saw that they hadn't followed him. He sighed with relief and resumed his walk back from the bathroom. Bruce yelped and stumbled backwards onto his butt. The two of them had materialized right before his eyes. He looked around but no one else was in the hallway with him. They didn't say anything but watched as Bruce got back to his feet, walked past them, and continued down the hall to where Lian was resting. He let himself in, saw that she was still wide awake and sat down beside her.

Bruce looked back at the couple, "See, I told you that she was awake."

Lian looked at him confused. "Who are you talking to?"

Bruce looked up at the couple who were now approaching her bed and then back to her.

"She can neither see nor hear us," the man said.

"Uh. No one. Just my inner demons," Bruce muttered. Lian cracked a small smile.

Bruce watched as the couple stood over Lian with sadness

in their eyes. They looked over at him pleadingly.

"Please help her." The woman implored.

"How?" Bruce asked.

"How what?" Lian asked him.

Bruce shook his head, "Sorry, thinking aloud." He gave Lian a weak smile before shooting a dirty look at the couple. "Rest up then I'll take you home."

Lian smiled and reached a hand out, tousling Bruce's hair. "Thank you for being here for me."

Bruce put her hand in his and kissed it gently. The couple looked at each other with hope flickering in their eyes before they evaporated into air.

A small village in Ireland

Fanai had talked with a few of the locals when he had first arrived. While they all sympathized with his amnesia none of them could offer any suggestions or solutions to help him get back his memories. The village had a doctor, but he was a medical doctor and not a psychologist. The nearest psychologist was more than a few hours away and the one thing that the locals all agreed on was that no 'head shrink' will help you remember anything until you've spent all of your money on them. And money was something Fanai had very little of.

When Fanai had first walked off the ferry he had only the address of the cabin to go by, the bag he had found in his hotel room, an empty wallet, and the ferry ticket stub. He had continued into the centre of town, asking around in attempts to find the address written on the scrap of paper he had found in his wallet. Fanai had gotten lucky when he wandered into Lucky Lucy's Tavern. Fanai asked the barkeep about the address and not only did the barkeep know where it was, but he knew who the manager of the cabin was and where the manager happened to be at that particular moment. It turned out that there was a small collection of cabins on the outskirt of town that were run by a man named Colin Murphy and Colin happened to be in the tavern, in a booth in the back, waiting, supposedly, for Fanai.

Fanai quietly slid into the booth. Colin was a large man with bright fiery red hair, fat stubby fingers and the thickest five o'clock shadow Fanai had ever seen this early on in the day. Colin was drinking a pint of Guinness and reading a newspaper. When Colin saw his guest had arrived he smiled, his grin revealing a mouthful of rotting old teeth. Colin folded his newspaper in half, set it to the side, waved a hand in the air and the barkeep brought over another pint of Guinness. When Fanai tried to refuse Colin chuffed and took a drink of his own beer.

"So, our lost boy has finally arrived," Colin said whole heartily.

Fanai looked at Colin with confusion. "Lost boy?" he asked.

Colin laughed, "I suppose you don't even remember the movie I'm referring too do you? It would be funny if you remembered that but had forgot the rest."

"Do I know you?" Fanai asked as Colin took another swig of his beer.

Colin slowly shook his head from side to side, "No lad, you don't. But someone does I reckon." He set his pint down, nodded his head towards Fanai and the lost boy begrudgingly took a drink. "Let me tell you a little story. About a year ago I got an email from an unnamed source requesting my assistance. They explained to me that in a years time, today in fact, they would require me to be at this tavern, at this exact time, and that I was to wait for someone whom was lost. Someone who had forgotten who they were, where they had come from and where they were to go. They didn't know what they would look like, if they were to be man, woman or child. Simply that they were lost and they would arrive on the 3:00 pm ferry. They requested a fully furnished cabin to be set up for said person, with the fridge fully stocked and they paid a years rent in advance. Once I set it all up and confirmed everything was as they had requested, they simply disappeared. Their email address no longer exists, the bank account that sent me the money no longer exists. Vanished without a trace, as if it had never even existed. So, I've been waiting for this day, to see if anyone would actually show up and here you are," Colin said brightly, his eyes twinkling.

Fanai stared at him incredulously and absently took another drink of his beer, finishing it in a single go.

"And you owe me a tenner now, don't ya?" the barkeep said and Colin waved him off as the barkeep roared with laughter.

"Its a bit of a wild tale, don't you think?" Colin started, "I hardly believed it myself. But here ya are and that piece of paper that you're clutching tightly in your hand has the address of the cabin that's already been paid for, doesn't it?" Fanai uncurled his clenched fist and flattened the paper out on the table in front of them. Colin nodded as he read it. "Do you have a name?" Colin asked.

Fanai shook his head from side to side.

"Do you know why you're here?" Colin asked.

Again, Fanai shook his head from side to side.

"Well I'll be darned. My wife is going to love this," Colin said with a chuckle, "A right up ole fan, aren't you? Drink up and I'll drive you out to your cabin." Fanai looked down and saw that a second pint had appeared in his hand and was already half empty. "I imagine you're travelling light?" Colin said motioning to the duffel bag on the bench next to Fanai.

Fanai picked up the beer and downed the rest of it in a single gulp. Colin laughed and slapped the table with his free hand. "Good lad, now lets git," he said as he stood up, dropping a few bills on the table.

Outside Colin led him to a small red pickup truck, barely the size of Volkswagen Beetle. Colin was chattering non-stop, pointing out areas of potential interest as they slowly drove through the village; a cafe, the grocery store, the bakery, and so on. Fanai tried to pay attention, but his mind was a jumble and he felt like he was sleep walking through a daydream. Fanai wasn't sure what bothered him the most; that someone knew who he was and wasn't helping him to figure it out, or that someone knew a year in advance that his memory would be lost to him.

They were already halfway out of town when with a start Fanai realized that he had unconsciously gotten into the truck, buckled up and that they were already on the outskirts of the village. Outside the village the small buildings were replaced with endless grassy fields where animals grazed and crops were scattered as far as the eye could see. Fanai could see a long grey stone wall that stood about a meter in height. It appeared to separate the two fields and he could see something resting on it. It was white with spatters of yellow dancing on it. A dress, maybe? As it blew softly in the wind Fanai found that he wasn't able to look away from it.

Lian rolled over and felt a tug at her arm. Her eyes blinked rapidly as they opened to the harsh glare of florescent lighting from either side of her cubicle. The light above her had been doused, but the curtains on either side only went so high and barely blocked the other lights from bleeding in. She looked down and saw the IV still inserted in her arm. The tube ran up to a machine, through it and to a now empty bag. The machine chirped softly and flashed a message of some kind. Probably telling the nurses that her bag had runs its course. Lian rolled over to her other side and saw Bruce, fast asleep, sitting in a chair beside her bed.

She looked around for her purse and found it on a tray between her and Bruce, sitting in front of a fresh bouquet of flowers. Leaning over, careful to not make any noise she pulled her purse onto her lap. As she did, she bumped the flowers and a card fell out. She grabbed it from the tray, expecting it be blank as it probably came from Bruce. But she was pleasantly surprised to see that it is was instead signed by Darin, with an apology for not being able to accompany her to the hospital. It said that he had felt Bruce was the better candidate as he appeared to have knowledge about her episode. Lian held the card close to her chest and smiled before slipping it into her purse.

She rummaged through her purse until she found her cell phone. Someone had thoughtfully turned it to vibrate and had also recently charged it. There were a couple of messages from Darin, again reiterating his apologies and offers of breakfast once she was discharged. Lian looked at the time and saw that it was six in the morning. She had been asleep for well over twelve hours. It had been late afternoon when she went shopping the day before. Bruce rustled in his sleep and she immediately froze. After what seemed like the longest minute in time she carefully put her purse back on the table, keeping her cell phone.

Lian looked over at Bruce, her heart torn. She had overheard the doctor telling Bruce that he was her medical legal guardian and the emotions had boiled up inside her. She wasn't surprised at what her adoptive parents had done, but she was upset that they had never told her. She had argued earlier with the doctor, begging him to remove Bruce as her guardian. The doctor had been sympathetic, but had insisted that Bruce remain as her guardian. In the events of her conditioning worsening to a state where she was unable to make medical decisions Lian needed to have someone present to do so, especially given her current condition. She had even begged him to let her choose someone else and was met with a frozen stare of apathy. He had scoffed and asked whom she would choose. He knew that Lian and Bruce were exchange students and he doubted that in four months time she had found someone who could step in that place. As he had pointed out, no one else was there in the hospital with her other than Bruce.

It was at that point Lian knew she was defeated and had immediately clammed up. The doctor had looked at her sorrowfully. She knew his hands were tied, but it didn't stop her from being upset. She was upset at a system that she wanted to be in, a system with rules and strictness that she adored — except at that particular moment.

Bruce abruptly sat up, mumbling and rubbing his eyes. She turned her back to him.

"Hey, you awake?" Bruce asked softly, touching her shoulder gently.

Lian remained silent, controlling her breathing, hoping that Bruce wouldn't come to the other side of the bed. He paced the small room, stretching his legs and arms as he did for a few minutes before sitting back down in the chair. As he did a doctor entered the room with a nurse following close behind. The nurse went for the IV and began the process of detaching it from her. In doing so she was forced to lay on her back and Bruce saw that she was wide awake. He looked over at her, concerned, but Lian focused her gaze on the doctor.

"Good morning Lian, my name is Doctor Buke. I've reviewed the notes from Doctor Graze and he has arranged a few more tests to be done this morning before we can discharge you," he said and she nodded numbly. The nurse disappeared briefly before returning with a wheelchair and placing it in front of Bruce.

"I'm fine," Bruce said confused and the nurse chuckled before leaving the room.

"Its for Lian," the doctor said, "Since you are her guardian we've deemed you responsible for getting her around to her various tests. That way you can finish up more quickly and get home sooner."

Lian immediately protested, insisting that she was fine and could walk. To prove so she swung her legs over the bed's edge and went to stand up. She felt her legs crumble beneath her and Bruce jumped to his feet, barely catching her before she could hit the ground. The doctor gave her a knowing look as Bruce set her gently in the wheelchair. Lian looked down at the ground, her face filled with embarrassment and misery, as the doctor grabbed her purse and the bouquet of flowers, handing them to Bruce.

"Follow me," he said and Bruce, pushing Lian, obliged.

Bruce and Lian exited the elevator estatic. It had been two weeks since she had been discharged from the hospital and it had been, from Bruce's perspective, a glorious time. With her lack of mobility and their year end exams coming up, the two of them had literally hibernated in their rooms studying with every spare minute they had. Lian had stopped locking her door and had even begun inviting him over to study together. They had just gotten the results of their mid semester exam, and despite everything that had been going on between them, they both scored in the high nineties. Bruce was still marvelling over the sudden turn in Lian's attitude towards him and was riding a personal high.

Their arms were linked as they skipped down the hallway to their rooms. Lian was singing *'Off to See the Wizard'* at the top of her lungs, dragging Bruce along as she did. He attempted to keep up with her skipping, but was constantly tripping over his own feet. They giggled as he stumbled about. By the time they got to the end of the hallway Lian was half carrying, half dragging Bruce.

As they reached their rooms Bruce suddenly stood upright and impulsively scooped Lian into his arms. She shrieked but let herself be carried, wrapping her arms around his neck. He tipped her over dramatically and she cried out in protest, clinging tightly to him. He briefly pause to steady himself while she pulled her keys out of her purse and unlocked her door. He kicked it open dramatically. Bruce barely managing to get Lian and himself through the doorway. Turning sideways he bumped her legs on the first attempt and her head on the second attempt. Lian laughed, teasing him that since she was tiny she should fit everywhere and she wasn't sure what he was doing wrong. He pretended to be hurt by her words, threatening to drop her. In one swift motion he dropped his arm, letting her legs fall out from beneath her. Lian's legs slammed into him, dangling in the air. Bruce's laughter died off quickly as he lowered Lian down to the ground. She clung to him as they observed, in silence, the chaos in her room.

The sheets had been torn from her bed and ripped into several pieces. Her mattress had been gutted and the insides had been stained a gruesome red. The contents of her closet were strewn about the room and several of them had been torn to pieces. The dresser drawers were pulled out and discard on the floor. What few dishes she had - a mug, a plate, and a glass - were shattered on the floor.

Bruce stood shellshocked amidst the clutter as Lian slowly made her way through the mess towards the bathroom. Her makeup and other beauty products were scattered about but not broken. She quietly opened the door to Bruce's room and saw that it bore a similar tornado-like look to hers. But after a quick look around Lian realized that it was his own personal tornado; nothing more. As she turned to go back to her room, she bumped into Bruce. She wrapped her arms around his broad chest and cried.

Chapter 9

A small village in Ireland

Fanai made the trek from his cabin on the outskirts of town to the inner parts of the village and back every day. He never left at the same time and often went to different destinations within the village. Sometimes Fanai went into town simply for supplies and sometimes to dine out. Most often he'd make his way into town, grab a coffee and a pastry then find a place to settle down with his sketchpad. Each time, regardless of whether it was morning, noon, or night, Fanai would see her off in the distance sitting on the stone fence in her white and pale yellow dress.

Fanai found himself as much drawn to her as he was afraid of her. He could never quite see her face clearly, nor could he even tell the colour of her hair even though he could clearly make out her white dress with pale yellow paisley flowers. She was always staring off into the fields; moving and not moving. Her dress was always fluttering about softly in the wind, even if there wasn't a breeze. Her face was always turned away from him. Just enough that Fanai felt as if she were avoiding his gaze. It was as if she was telling him she would not come to him and that Fanai needed to come to her. While she would not acknowledge him, it seemed that she would stay and wait for him for however long it may take.

These were thoughts that danced in his mind as Fanai walked both in and out of town each day. The thoughts were nothing more than those of an old foolish man. He never called out to her. He never waved, nor attempted to stop and take a good look at her. She was nothing more than a tree in the background of the scenery in his day to day life. And yet, she seemed to be the most important thing in it.

Each day Fanai would find somewhere new to sketch. He felt that if he tried to sketch normal things he might stumble upon a lost memory. Perhaps he could draw something that he once knew and unlock a clue to his past. But, no matter what he first gazed upon, no matter what he tried to draw, it always became her. It became the girl in the white and yellow paisley dress. The girl with the sad eyes.

When Fanai had woken up that morning, he told himself that today was the day that he would try to introduce himself to her. At the very least he would stop and wave hello. Perhaps he would even shout out a greeting. Yet on his walk into town, as he grew closer and closer to the stone fence. He dug his hands deeper into his pockets and lowered his gaze to the ground, hunching over. Fanai felt as if that would hide him from her. The closer he got to the fence the quicker his pace grew, until finally she and the fence were far behind him. Fanai then stood up straight and let out a huge breath of air that he hadn't realize he was holding in. As he did a soft chuckle came was heard from behind him. Without even a backwards glance Fanai broke off in a mad dash and ran the rest of the way to the village.

Later that evening, much later than he had ever left before, Fanai finally made his way down the familiar path back home. Fanai told himself that he didn't want to cook that evening, so he could stay in the pub and have a decent meal. The truth was Fanai was afraid to walk past her again. He knew that she was the one who had laughed at him. That she was waiting for him. But Fanai figured that there was no way she was outside at this hour. Not only was it dark, but it was also quite cold. He found himself chilled to the bone in the light summer jacket he had put on when he left earlier that morning.

As Fanai trudged his way down the path he could feel his sketchbook weighing heavily upon him. Several times during the day he had found himself opening the book and beginning to sketch her. Each time he caught himself and immediately slammed the book shut. His heart shuddered at the thought of seeing her again. He had started tearing out the pages already filled with her image, but then stopped himself. His heart ached as he crumpled the pages. He unwillingly began to smooth them out again; stuffing them back inside the sketchpad.

The buildings quickly gave way to the fields and Fanai's heart leapt into his throat. He scolded himself, no little girl could harm him and he was foolish to think otherwise. Why was he letting himself get so caught up in these foolish emotions? Besides, Fanai reminded himself, there was no way that she would be out there at this late hour.

And yet, as Fanai rounded the corner before the stone fence, he could hear the soft fluttering of her dress in the wind. Even in the darkness of the night, Fanai could see her dress blowing gently. His throat grew dry and he found it difficult to swallow. His feet grew heavier as if they were filling with lead with each step that he took. Her back was to him and he wondered briefly if she always sat that way, with her back to him. Part of him could swear that she was always facing him, no matter which direction he came from. He thought he would feel relief, but there was something incredibly intimidating about approaching her from behind. He felt that at any given moment she would suddenly turn around and no longer be a woman, but a monster waiting to eat him alive.

Fanai shook his head, trying to clear it of the nonsensical thoughts that were rambling about inside before he realized that he had stopped at the end of the fence. In fact, his hands were touching the fence. It was same stone fence that she sat upon. Fanai looked down at his hands, alarmed and mesmerized. His gaze slowly went from his hands to the the fence beneath them, then up along the fence, slowly making his way towards her. Voices were screaming inside his head, telling himself to stop, but he was no longer in control of his body. Every fibre within screamed at him, telling him to run. They told him to let go. To run. Fanai could feel tears welling up in the corners of his eyes and yet, he couldn't stop himself from staring at her.

Finally, his gaze fell upon her dress. His heart leapt again as his eyes made their way up her waist, her chest, her arms, her neck and finally her head. Her hair was jet black, with streams of red and purple intertwined within them. The red and purple weren't hair, but more like streams of soft light attempting to resemble hair. They too, flowed in the windless air, much like an anime character's would. He could see that her skin was pale white, her lips a light pink and her eyes a vibrant blue-green. Like him, there were tears welling up in the corners of her eyes. His breath drew in sharply and he gasped as she ever so subtly, turned her head toward him. Her eyes, still downcast, blinked slowly. Her eyelids opened and her pupils slowly rolled up, until her eyes met his. Her eyes were filled with sadness. She no longer looked upon the field but was focused entirely upon him. As quickly as she had looked upon his face, she turned back to the fields and a single tear rolled down her cheek.

Bruce and Lian had just delivered a patient to the hospital and were en route towards the nearest cafe. Their shift, part of their courses' curriculum, had a little over an hour left in it and they both were starving. With the holidays approaching, Lian was craving a Starbucks turkey cranberry sandwich that you could only buy during Christmas in Canada. She had been talking about it all day and they both hoped to find something similar as neither of them had been able to take a break during their shift. Normally, as students, they worked with a supervisor which would allow them to have staggered breaks. But there was an unusual shortage of paramedics supervisors that day and they were one of two pairings allowed to work unsupervised.

As their luck would have it, the day had been insanely hectic. They had barely finished their pre-shift checks when multiple calls came in and all units were immediately dispatched. Since their first call that morning, they had been going none stop. First an elderly woman with a personal emergency response system had needed assistance followed by a trip to the hospital. Then there was an overdose at a local high school, a car accident, and lastly an office worker had fallen from a ladder as a result of a mild heart attack. And that was just them. The phones had been ringing off the hook all day.

Using the app on her phone Lian placed an order at the nearest Starbucks. As Bruce rounded the corner she hopped out of the ambulance and ran inside to grab their order. As Lian disappeared inside dispatch crackled through the radio. Bruce grabbed his receiver and called in.

The dispatch crackled, "We have a 12-67 with a possible 10-9. Police are requesting ambulance backup. Are you still within the vicinity of St. Georges Hospital? Over."

Bruce copied and wrote down the address on the scribble pad next to the radio. By the time Lian returned he had found the address on the GPS. She had barely strapped herself in when Bruce turned on the siren, pulled the vehicle back into oncoming traffic and raced down the street.

Bruce looked at her grimly, "This isn't going to be pretty." Lian looked at him with concern as she tried to swallow the bite of her sandwich already in her mouth.

Ten minutes later they arrived at the scene of the incident. Several police cars were situated outside of the house. As Bruce pulled up they saw police officers escorting a handcuffed couple into the back of one of the cars. Before Bruce could come to a complete stop Lian slid the side door open, hopped out with a full medical kit in hand, and dashed off into the house. Bruce put the ambulance in park and grabbed the oxygen tank and defibrillator before following her inside.

As Lian entered through the open front door she called out to the police officers inside. They shouted at her to come upstairs. Lian raced up the stairs upon hearing the urgency in their voices. A police officer was standing at the doorway and pointed inside.

Inside was a child's room, a girl's room Lian had thought at first, until she saw the young boy lying down on the floor. His skin was waxy and pale and he was laying in a large pool of blood. Two police officers were kneeling down beside him, one officer was pressing a towel against the boy's upper thigh. The other held a towel on his stomach.

"What happened?" Lian asked as she visually assessed the situation while putting a pulse oximeter on the boy's pointer finger. She checked his pulse on his carotid artery and kept check on her watch. His pulse was a mere 40 beats per minute. His heart was failing. The officers explained quickly how the child was a victim of extreme violent outbursts from both of his parents.

Lian opened her bag as Bruce entered the room. She told him to have the defibrillator on standby. She passed Bruce a roll of heavy duty gauze and he began to inspect the area around the towel for leaking blood. Satisfied that he saw none, Bruce put a dressing on the boys leg and secured it over the towel with the gauze. Lian had just cut the remainder of the boys' dress as he began to sob. Lian smiled and reassured the boy that they could fix the dress up no problem, but they had to fix him first. The boy tried to smile back at her, but could only muster a small lift at the edges of his lips.

Bruce, still dressing the boys arm, watched as everything inside the room suddenly began to slow down. The boy slowly raised his arm, the one closest to Lian, as she leaned over to examine his face more closely. He gently place his hand onto her cheek. The air had grown thick and heavy and Bruce found it difficult to breathe. Even more perplexing was that no one else seemed to notice the change in time. Bruce watched as Lian leaned in even closer so the boy could whisper something into her ear. He tried to shout out, telling her to move away, to not listen. White tendrils of light grew out of her hand and reached out towards the young boy. A single tear slide down Lian's cheek, glistening as bright as the morning sun on dew drops.

Time abruptly resumed normally and the boys arm fell down lifelessly, smearing blood down Lian's cheek and hitting the ground with a loud thud. His eyes rolled back and his mouth fell slack. The white tendrils evaporated as Lian's eyes briefly held a void of hope and life. Her eyes grew darker until there was nothing left but pupils. Her encouraging smile slipped away into a lifeless and slack pout. Bruce called out to Lian but his voice came out slurred, heavy, and distorted. He fought the thickness of the air between them, trying to reach his hand out to comfort her. But before he could Lian pushed herself away from the boy, her eyes growing as wide as saucers and her mouth opened in a silent scream. The sheer terror in her eyes terrified him. Lian was looking directly at Bruce, but couldn't see him.

Then, just as suddenly, the spell was broken. The invisible foggy thickness was gone from the air and Bruce could hear himself speak normally again. Lian was huddled in a corner of the room, screaming. He reached out towards her but felt the boy between them. He closed his eyes, said a quick prayer and immediately turned his attention to the probably already dead boy beneath him. He did his best to push Lian's screams out of his head as he pulled out the defibrillator and tried to save the boys life. Because Bruce knew, that at this particular moment, there was nothing he could do for her.

They were back at the dorms. Bruce had just put Lian in her bed. She was shivering. Her skin was cool to the touch and sticky with perspiration. Bruce stripped her out of her clothes, down to her undergarments and Lian just sat there obediently like a small helpless child. She laid down as he pulled the blankets over her. She stared blankly at the ceiling, her eyes wide and unblinking. He disappeared for a few minutes only to return with a mug of hot water and lemon. He sat down beside her and held the mug out. Her gaze moved slightly towards the mug and then back to the ceiling. He sighed as he set the mug down, pulled her up into a seated position, and brought the mug to her lips. She took the mug with her hands that trembled slightly. Bruce grabbed her pills from the bathroom but she shrugged her head. He took one out regardless and set it on the nightstand beside her.

"What the hell happened Lian?" Bruce asked. Lian continued to stare absently at the wall. He couldn't tell if she was faking it or not. He took her by the shoulders, turned her to face him, and shook her. "I'm serious. This is legitimately scaring me. You need to cut this crap out or I'll drag you back to the hospital myself," he said sternly.

Lian blinked rapidly as the colour began to return to her cheeks. She exhaled deeply and coughed. She set the mug down on the night stand. She opened her mouth to say something but quickly shut it and looked away from him.

"You're lucky it was just the two of us. If our supervisor was with us and saw how you reacted you'd be expelled on the spot." Lian continued to look away from him. "Please. Lian, c'mon. Please tell me something, anything," Bruce begged of her.

"I'm sorry," Lian mumbled. "I — I —" she wailed as she fell face first onto her pillow, trying to muffle her sobs. Bruce grabbed her by the shoulders and turned her over to face him. She cried out and struggled to free herself from him, but his grip held tight.

"What -" Bruce started, "what is going on with you?" His voice wavered slightly as he tried to hide his fear from her. "This isn't the first time this has happened, is it?" he asked.

She continued to sob uncontrollably and could only choke out half mumbled words.

"Lian, please let me help you." He tried pleading with her but she only continued to cry. Letting her go she pulled herself into a ball beneath the covers. Bruce gave her one last look before standing up and walking into his bedroom. He slammed the door behind him.

Bruce's shoes pounded on the ground with heavy slaps as he made his way through the trails behind the campus. His breath was frosty and his heart began to race as he started up the hill. The trees engulfed him, giving him the solitude he so desperately needed. Bruce was at his wits end. Lian was fading away a little bit at a time with each passing day and there was nothing he could do to help.

Lian's attacks were increasing and her health was deteriorating rapidly. She was aggressively pushing him away and only reluctantly letting him help her when she had no other options. Bruce was tired of being held at arms length. He hadn't seen her ghost parents in weeks and was waffling on the fact that he had fabricated their existence to help justify his desires. The doctors could find nothing else wrong with Lian, to the point of bafflement. She was obviously ill but all of the tests came back negative. Bruce hated feeling so helpless and frustrated. He knew that Lian was hiding something. Whether or not she was hiding it from herself was another story. It was much like her ghost parents hiding the truth from him. Bruce was growing tired of being a pawn in their games.

Looking up Bruce saw the path split into two. On one side he could make out a large tree just off the side of a path. He felt his heart tug slightly as he realized how much it resembled the tree that held his and Lian's treehouse back home. He turned himself onto that path, curious about the tree. Further up he could see a figure at the top of the hill. As Bruce got closer to the top he realized it was a couple but neither looked dressed for running. His heart jumped into his throat when realized who they were. He picked up his pace, afraid that they might vanish on him again. Bruce pushed himself up the hill and forced himself to fight the pain in his side. He could see the sadness in their eyes and their longing for peace and rest.

When Bruce reached them he was out of breath. He hunched over putting his hands on his knees and began sucking in the cold air in deep shrilly breaths. Although they were unable to physically touch him Bruce could feel the woman's hand as it settled just above his shoulder. They waited until Bruce was standing upright before looking him in the eyes.

"She needs your help now."

"More than ever."

"With what? Exams? Sorry we just finished those," Bruce said with haughtiness in his voice. He hadn't intended to come across as an ass, but the anger just poured out of him.

They looked at each other and exchanged sympathetic glances before looking back at him. "We cannot say," they said in unison.

"I don't know how you expect me to help her when you won't even tell me what is wrong with her. What happens if I don't help her? Does the world end?" Bruce said exasperated, throwing his hands up in the air in frustration.

"Everything will end."

"Not just your world."

Bruce slowly put his arms down, "Everything?"

"There is much more out there, more than you can ever imagine. You are not alone. Just the last," he said.

"You can't let it end like this. She cannot help herself. She isn't…she isn't herself. She's lost, confused, and scared."

"But she doesn't know yet. She won't know until its too late."

"Then how am I supposed to help her?"

"Make her remember."

"Wake her up."

"How?"

They looked at each other again with defeat. "We don't know how."

"Christ, you're bloody useless then aren't you?" Bruce mumbled to himself under his breath. He took in a deep breath and slowly exhaled it. "Why is Lian so important?"

"There is much we cannot tell you, for it is not ours to say. But we can tell you that she is important to us. Very important."

"She is our daughter."

Bruce inhaled sharply. "She's really not human, is she?" he said softly, his voice not much more than a mere whisper.

"She is for now."

"But she won't be forever."

"She must return to what she really is."

"What is she? Who are you?" Bruce cried out, frustrated.

The couple looked at each other silently and then back at Bruce. He eyed them suspiciously.

The man bowed his head slightly. "They called me Eld. And she, my partner, is called Auld."

"We are Eldrossian." Auld said quietly.

Bruce grew quiet. He hadn't expected an actual answer from them. He began to walk away from them but turned back. "Why is Lian human now? Why not forever? Will she change when she's not human? Why should I even help her? Why me?" Bruce spouted his questions like an overflowing water fountain.

Auld reached her hand out towards Bruce and put it on his shoulder. She flickered like a signal being lost and looked at the man with fear. She looked back at Bruce frantically. "We may not be able to come to you again. Our time here is almost over. Save her. Save our daughter," she begged as they both disappeared in the blink of an eye.

Chapter 10

The room was pounding with loud music and was jammed packed with students. People were draped over the staircase going upstairs and hanging out the windows. Not a single nook or cranny was unoccupied. There was a group of guys doing shots in one corner while another group sat on the couch getting stoned. The lights flickered briefly and then shut off. The music went silent. A large groan filled the house and someone booed. Then the lights flickered back on and the room was suddenly filled with a variety of multicoloured disco lighting. The students erupted with cheers and laughter as the music resumed.

Lian held gingerly onto Darin's jacket. He had offered her his hand when they walked up the stairwell but she had pretended not to notice. As they entered the house she felt small and was instantly overwhelmed. His hand was nowhere to be found so she settled for his jacket sleeve instead. She wondered if she made a mistake coming as they made their way through the crowd and into the kitchen. Darin took Lian by the arm and led her to a table covered with a smattering of alcohol and mixers. He whipped up a couple of drinks while she surveyed the crowd.

Lian could see Bruce on the other side of the kitchen surrounded by his fan club. Bruce tried to catch her attention, shooting her a confused look as she looked away and buried her face in Darin's broad shoulder. Darin handed her a drink, took Lian by the arm and guided her out of the kitchen, directly past Bruce. Darin grinned like the Cheshire cat at Bruce. Bruce glared back. Lian was too preoccupied with avoiding Bruce's gaze to notice. As they made their way through the crowd she felt as if everyone was giving them a wide berth. Everyone was polite. They stopped every couple of feet to talk to someone new. For once people were actually acknowledging her in a positive manner. Perhaps Lian was just being paranoid she thought to herself.

Darin handed Lian his drink and excused himself to go find some of the mythical pizza he had just heard about. She took his drink and nodded finding herself hovering too closely to the couch that reeked of pot. She settled herself back against the wall giving herself an excellent vantage point to the chaos around her with the cover of the stoners smokey haze to hide her. She took a sip of her drink and looked around for a nearby seat that she could snag. A pretty blonde with too much money and not enough fashion sense for the winter popped up out of nowhere. She wore hot pants and a tube top under a see through white blouse that was mostly unbuttoned. As Lian was discreetly looking over the girl's outfit she realized that the girl was looking her over too.

"He's not with me, he's been cornered by the rest of your flock," Lian said casually, pointing towards the kitchen.

The girl laughed, "We don't want him, we came to talk to you," she said with an annoying girly laugh. Lian noticed a small entourage of girls had gathered around her. She raised her eyebrows in disbelief as the blonde stuck her hand out in front of her. Hesitantly, she went to take it, but her arm jerked involuntarily. She flushed bright red as the girls giggled.

"Burn. Weirdo," Lian heard them mutter.

The blonde smiled firmly, ignoring their comments and grabbed Lian's hand, shaking it vigourously. "My name is Sarah. This is Jess, Trudy, Steffie, Sam, and Rebecca," she said introducing the girls around her. "We're sorry we've gotten off on the wrong foot with you. We shouldn't have expected you to know the way things work here and we understand that things might be different back home in Canada," Sarah said with a flourish. She batted her eyelashes for dramatic emphasis.

Lian downed the remainder of her drink swiftly and gave them a smile which she hoped didn't look as fake as it felt. She took a big gulp of Darin's drink and eyed the girls carefully. She knew that they couldn't be trusted, but she felt herself having trouble concentrating. Sarah was the ring leader of the Bruce fan club. Lian bit her lip, stifling a giggle as the thought of them being more like Japanese high school girls than Swiss bitches crossed her mind.

"Thank you for your apology. It means a lot to me," Lian said quietly, her mind endeavouring to think rapidly. She knew she had to get away from them before they noticed that she was spacing out. Lian didn't know what was coming over her, but she needed solitude quickly. She held her plastic cups up and shook them to indicate they were empty. Lian shrugged her shoulders with a smile and tried excuse herself to go find another drink. One of the girls snatched the cups from her hands and ran off with a skip in the direction of the kitchen.   She tried to grab her cups back but Sarah grabbed her arm and firmly held it down. Sarah slowly shook her head no and told her to let her new friends help her. Lian looked at Sarah with sincere disbelief. Friends? One apology made them friends? She shook her head trying to clear it, uncertain of what she was actually hearing compared to what she thought she was hearing. Her mind was growing quite foggy and the party felt like it was growing distant.

Sarah began to prattle on about Bruce and how since Lian was Bruce's close friend, she could be a great friend to them by sharing everything that she knew about Bruce. Lian laughed aloud. She wondered why none of the girls had bothered to interrogate her like this in the first place. She would have been more than happy to answer questions about Bruce. Especially if it had meant that they wouldn't have harassed her. Hell, she would have volunteered the information from the get go if she knew they would leave her alone. Lian knew that he should have a girlfriend. Bruce needed someone to distract him from her.

Lian smiled brightly, not realizing that Sarah and her posse were leading her around the house. They waved to people as they passed and at some point a drink had appeared in her hand and then one for the other. She was just at the story of Bruce's big fumble during the most important game of the year when she realized that they were standing outside in the backyard, in the freezing cold. Lian took a step back and turned full circle. The girls were gone and only Sarah remained with her hands on her hips.

"Guess trashing your room wasn't enough of a hint, was it?" Sarah said smugly. "Perhaps this will give you some time to think things through and realize that Bruce is mine."

Sarah stepped inside the house and closed the kitchen door, locking it behind her. A cruel smile played on Sarah's lips as she half closed the blinds on the door. Lian walked towards the door but only got a few steps when she was suddenly whipped off her feet and fell face first into the hard packed snow.

She pushed her upper body up off the ground and touched her face gingerly. Her left ankle throbbed and she realized that it had been attached to a chain that was secured to a post behind her. She shook her leg and it rattled loudly. Lian could see Sarah laughing at her thru the window as she waggled a key in front of her face. Sarah pocketed it, closed the blinds the rest of the way and then disappeared into the depths of the house.

Lian stared at the back door flabbergasted. She had figured they were up to something with the fake apology, but had assumed they had just wanted to pump her for information. She hadn't expected this. She sat up on her knees and examined her face. She found a bit of blood under her nose that had already froze to her skin. She heard the music increase in volume, followed by loud ruckus cheering. Lian sighed, knowing that any attempts at yelling for help would be futile. She searched for her cell phone and sighed, remembering that she had left it in her jacket pocket which one of the girls took from her. She raised a hand to her temple and moaned softly. Her head was heavy and she could feel her insides swimming about. She wondered what kind of alcohol Darin had put in the drinks. Apparently the Swedes had a much higher tolerance than she did.

Lian pulled herself up into a squatting position and wrapped her arms around her legs, pulling them tight to her chest. She was already starting to shiver. She wondering how long they intended to leave her out here and how long it would take for Darin to realize that she was missing or if he would even notice. He seemed to be as much as a social bunny as Bruce was. She'd only been outside a few minutes and she could barely feel her fingers. It was well below zero. Her training told her that any more than an hour out here and her body would begin to freeze.

A small village in Ireland

The rain hammered down on Fanai's roof and the walls

shuddered from the force of the gusting wind. The windows rattled in place as the wind howled against them, trying to force its way in. A small fire crackled in the corner of the room, embers snapping cheerfully as he stoked the fire with an old cast iron rod. Fanai shuffled his way - wearing flannel pyjamas, a large cardigan type sweater, and grandma style pink fluffy slippers - towards the kitchen area, eager for his morning cup of coffee.

Lightening struck. His lights flickered on and off a few times before coming back on again. Fanai stopped and looked up at the ceiling, as if he could magically see through the roof. A few seconds later thunder rumbled filling the air. He grabbed a dirty mug out of the sink and quickly rinsed it off. The rain pelted heavily against the window that sat above the sink. Big raindrops smushed against it and slid down quickly, like fat blobs of ice cream melting down a waffle cone on a hot summer day. He quickly poured the coffee into the mug, took a large swig, and began a hunt for candles.

He got lucky on his first guess. The top middle drawer of the kitchen island held not only candles, but several candle holders and matches. Carefully, he heated the bottoms of each candle and pressed them firmly into place, each in their respective holder. Once they were all seated and the wax solid again, he lit them all, one by one. As Fanai lit the last candle, lightening struck again, this time thunder followed much more quickly than the last. The lights flickered once more before falling dark. He chuckled as he took another drink of his coffee. He rummaged in his cardigan pocket, found some rum and added a rather large splash to his coffee. He took another drink and smiled fondly.

Fanai hovered above the candles, his reflection causing shadows to dance wildly on the walls as he listened to the rainfall. He closed his eyes and immediately he saw her. He wondered if she was out there in the rain. Part of him speculated that no one in their right mind would be out in this weather. But she had been out in the cold evening before and her mind may or may not entirely be there. Fanai shook his head in attempt to clear his thoughts of her. He had work to do and didn't need the distraction. One of the villagers had commissioned him to draw up sketches of their children in a fairy tale like story. He had already picked out the story he wanted to loosely follow and had assigned each child to a character in his mind. Now he only need to do the real work.

He moved the candles over by the sitting chair near the fireplace. On one side of the chair stood a table and he placed several candles on it. With a single candle in hand he wandered the room until he found another table and placed it on the other side of the chair. After dispersing the candles as efficiently as possible, he topped up his coffee on both accounts and grabbed his sketchbook. Fanai flipped to the first page addressed with a post-it note. He read his scribbles and began to sketch out two little boys playing in a field in the background while an even younger girl played by herself.

He quickly finished the basis of the first page and flipped over to the next. He read the post-it note, thought for a moment or two and then began to sketch. He alternated between sketching, drinking coffee, and stoking the fire. He stopped only once to refill his coffee and to move wood closer to the fire. The morning had quickly turned into the afternoon and only when his stomach rumbled louder than the storm outside did Fanai realize how late in the day it had already become. Still holding his sketchbook he grabbed one of the candle stubs that was still lit and wandered over to the kitchen. He made himself a sandwich and opened the sketchbook on the kitchen island. He began flipping through the pages, admiring his work, spotting areas to fix and made some little changes. Fanai was halfway through his sketches when he finally noticed her face. It was small, almost unnoticeable, but it was there.

He gasped softly. He turned to the next sketch and after a few minutes he found her face hidden in it. Almost like a creepy version of Where's Waldo. He flipped sketch by sketch until he made his way to the end and in each and every one he found at least one, sometimes two, small sketches of her face hidden inside. He turned to a blank page, almost expecting her face to suddenly appear and stare him down accusingly. As if asking him why he hadn't come to her yet. Why he letting her suffer in the rain alone.

Instinctively Fanai began to draw. He drew the stone fence that she sat on, then the grass that lay beneath her feet, and then her foot. Slowly but surely he made his way up her legs, her dress, and her waist. Like the day he first made eye contact with her he fought against himself. He was terrified of what her eyes may say to him. Only this time she wasn't staring him down. She was gazing off into the distance. Her hair, despite the torrential rain, was still soft, light, and flowing in the imaginary wind. Her dress also remained dry, crisp and clean. It flowed as freely as her hair. Rain drops fell around her but none touched her. And yet, you could see that rain wasn't falling on her.

Fanai sighed and turned the page. He couldn't stop himself. Her drew her face. He drew her eyes, her smile, the sadness that lay beneath them. He drew the softness of her skin, the light airiness of her hair, and the sparkle in her eyes that hid beneath the pain. He drew her pale pink lips; her smooth porcelain like skin; and her black eyelashes that went on for days. When he finished her face he turned to another blank page and drew her again. And again and again. His fingers cried out in pain as his grip on the pencil grew tighter and tighter. Finally, his head collapsed into his hands. He lay his head onto the sketchbook and sobbed.

* * *

Bruce, as usual, was surround by a bevy of women. They were laughing at his jokes and lightly touching his arms. He knew that he should be happy at the attention he was getting, but he felt empty inside. He looked around the room again trying to spot Lian. He hadn't expected to see her at the party, let alone with Darin. His heart felt crushed when he saw the two of them together. Even though it was quickly becoming a reoccurring thing. Lian never brought Darin over and she came home every night alone, but she spent less and less time at the dorms and Bruce was reeling inside over the prospect of the two of them together.

Bruce chugged the rest of his drink, smiling as he belched out loud and excused himself to find another drink. He sighed silently as the girls giggled at his belching. Nothing he did repulsed them. It was pitiful how shallow and empty headed these girls were. They only cared about how he looked and that he was *shiny and new*. He didn't care for a trophy wife, he wanted someone with as much, if not more, brains as looks. He wanted Lian.

He pushed his way through the crowds waving his empty cup about like a torch in the air, taking the long route towards the kitchen. He was halfway down the stairs when Sarah, aka el diablo, he thought to himself, appeared in front of him. She took his cup out of his hand and placed a fresh cup, filled to the brim with beer, in its place. Sarah smiled like the cat that just ate the canary and took his arm in hers.

"I've been looking all over for you," Sarah said as she lead him up the stairs.

Bruce resisted and turned back down the stairs. Out of the corner of his eye, he saw Darin without Lian. Perhaps this was his chance to catch a moment with her.

"Really? Why am I not surprised?" Bruce replied, his words dripping with sugar. Sarah irked him the most of all the girls that fawned over him. She actually had brains yet preferred to act like a bimbo in the public eye. He scanned the crowd again before Sarah could pull his attention back.

"You're not going to find her," Sarah said sweetly.

Bruce looked at her suspiciously, "Where is she?"

"Lian's not feeling well so she's lying down for a bit. Poor thing has a terrible headache."

Bruce looked around the room and saw Darin chatting up a couple of girls. His arm was around the waist of one of them and the other girl was leaning in close, her hands on his chest. Darin pecked the one girl on the cheek. Bruce glared at him and pushed his way down the stairs.

"Don't mind him. Not worth your time," Sarah purred, grabbing him by the arm and guiding him back up the stairs.

"I want to see her," Bruce insisted.

"Don't be silly, she's asleep by now," Sarah said. "I've been looking for you for almost a half hour now."

Bruce looked at her with doubt. "Why would you be looking for me and not her date?"

"She didn't come with you?" Sarah asked innocently. "How strange. I just assumed she had." Bruce relaxed slightly and Sarah smiled with approval. She squeezed his arm tightly and led him up the stairs. "Why don't you tell me more about Canada," Sarah said as she walked them into a bedroom at the top of the stairs.

Bruce relaxed a little more and began to tell her about Canada as she closed the door behind him. As she did he slammed her up against the door. She giggled and sighed happily.

"I do like to play it rough, but never thought you were the type."

Bruce leaned in close to her, their lips almost touching. "Where the hell is she?"

Sarah went to feign innocence but the look in Bruce's eyes terrified her. She felt herself shrinking beneath his hand on her sternum, which now held her firmly against the door.

Lian slowly opened her eyes, batting her partially frozen eyelashes. Snow fluttered off of her face. She rubbed her eyes of what she thought was sleep, which was actually ice crystals. She was now leaning against the post. She was unsure of how long she had been outside or when she had fallen asleep. Lian remembered that she had tried making snowballs and throwing them at the house. But she was too far away to even reach the back porch. She had kept trying until her fingers could no longer move. Then she had tried to jimmy the cuff locked around her ankle with her hair barrettes. The movies made it look like such an easy task, but she had only succeeded in breaking her barrettes. Then she followed the chain to the post and tried to remove the post. Sometime after that she must have fallen asleep.

The party inside was still in full swing. Lian looked up into the sky. It was still a crystal clear night. She could navigate her way through the woods but she had no idea how to see passage of time by the stars. Looking back at the house she could feel the rage welling up inside her as she began to convulse. She began to frantically pull at the chain, tears forming in her eyes and freezing almost as quickly as they appeared. The tears pulled at her skin, scratching and irritating it. She cried out in frustration and choked back the sobs. She lost control of herself as full panic set in and she screamed, fighting fruitlessly against the chain. She knew that she was starting to develop hypothermia and was going into shock, but she couldn't help herself.

With one last cry Lian fell to the ground in a heap, sobbing. She lay on her side, her body curled up in a tight ball, her hands clawing at the snow beside her. She picked up more snow, but it melted in her hands. Puzzled, she looked at the water now dripping out of her hand. She put her hand on top of some nearby snow, which felt cool to the touch. But it quickly melted beneath her hand. Lian laughed as she realized that she could now feel the snow beneath her body melting. She began to laugh hysterically and cry at the same time as she could feel a puddle of water forming beneath her.

Lian heard the back door slam open and the loud beats of music pour outside. Suddenly she could hear Bruce's voice calling out to her. She lifted her fingers slightly off the ground, her whole arm trembling as it hovered a couple of inches above the ground. She tried to lift her head up and call out to him, but her voice cracked and she could only whisper his name. Tears flowed freely down her face. Lian could hear Bruce's voice getting closer to her.

Bruce stopped a couple of feet away from her and stood shellshocked at the sight before him. She lay on the ground, her leg chained to a post. He barely noticed that Lian was laying in a circle of unmelted snow even though a perfect six foot diameter circle encompassed her like a crop circle in a field of snow. Bruce knelt down beside Lian and shook her gently until she finally answered him. She smiled weakly at him before passing out again. He roared with anger and looked back towards the house where a small group of students now gathered at the sight of him inside the snow crop circle.

Bruce yelled at them to get blankets, to call 9-1-1, and to bring him bolt cutters. He pulled Lian in close and wrapped his arms around her, trying to warm her. He rubbed her body vigorously as he held her close. A timid voice from within the crowd asked if he wanted the key. Bruce looked up, his face in an angry snarl.

"If the bastards who did this actually have the balls to face me then bring me the key!" Bruce said through gritted teeth.

A young girl stepped out of the crowd and rushed over to Bruce. "A group of girls just ran out of the house and threw this at me," she said as she handed him the key. "I know who they are."

Once Lian was unlocked Bruce lifted her into his arms and stood up. Another student came out with a blanket and they wrapped her in it as he walked back into the house. Most of the students followed Bruce inside while a few remained outside, lingering at the miraculous oddity of a perfect circle in the snow.

Chapter 11

The blaring of the alarm brought Bruce out of his restless slumber. He groaned and rolled over, his arm flopping over the edge of his bed. He felt it slap against something soft and heard a feminine grunt. He peered over and saw Lian, still asleep, at the side of his bed. He sighed and rolled onto his back. She had been all clingy when they left the party, but at the hospital she had pushed him away again. It had gotten so bad that he had debated on leaving her to fend for herself. But he had sucked it up and gotten her home. Immediately she locked her side of the bathroom door so he passed out in his bed.

He carefully stepped over her and went into her room. He heard the coffee pot begin to brew and laughed. No matter how difficult, stubborn or how tired she may be she always had her coffee set to brew in the morning. He knew that her alarm would be going off shortly so he scooped her up into his arms and carried her back into her room. En route she woke up and began to freak out. She fought against him as he tried to gently put her down and ended up dropping her entirely. She squeaked as she hit the ground.

"What the hell is your problem Lian?"

"You're my problem. You're always all over me," she retorted. Her eyes flaring as she gingerly rubbed her bottom.

"Me? You're the one who crawled over to my room. I was merely returning her highness to her throne."

She stared him with a loss for words and reluctantly got to her feet. She stomped past him, further into his room, to investigate his claims. As she did, he helped himself to a cup of her coffee. She returned to her room. Her face was a mixture of anger and despair.

"That's my coffee," she said trying to pull it out of his hands. He held the cup above his head, well out of her reach.

"What are you five? You always make half a pot. Given your piss poor gratitude I think I've earned it." He took a sip and wandered back into his room, slamming his bathroom door shut. He sat down on his bed, took another sip of his coffee and lay back.

After a few moments his bathroom door creaked open. "Bruce?" Lian stood in the doorway with her own mug. "Can I come in?"

"That depends. Are you going to take it out on me again or act like a normal human being?"

She lingered at the door, unable to answer.

He sighed, sat up and patted the space beside him. "Come in, come in. Have a seat."

She pulled the chair from his desk out and sat down. Awkward silence filled the room as they sipped their coffees. Finally she spoke. "I'm sorry."

"For what specifically? There are many things you could be sorry for," he said a little too sharply.

She winced at his words, stood up as if to leave then sat back down. "I feel like we're drifting apart," she started. Lian stared wistfully across the room, afraid to make eye contact with him.

"Only one drifting is you."

She looked down at the floor, her face growing warm. She put her coffee on the desk, got up, and crossed the room to sit down beside him. He didn't budge as she leaned her head on his shoulder.

"We've been friends since we were born. I don't want to lose that," she paused briefly and glanced up at him. His usually cheerful face was unreadable. "You mean the world to me."

He rubbed his face with one hand and held his breath. "Doesn't really feel like that these days to be perfectly honest."

"I know. I'm sorry. I really am. I'm just, so confused right now." Lian started to cry and instinctively Bruce put his arm around her shoulder and squeezed.

He put a hand to her forehead. "You're quite warm. How do you feel?"

"Like I need a cold shower and a fresh coffee." She gave a lopsided smile.

"Seriously."

"I'm fine. Just a little tired," she insisted as he looked her over. "Are we good?"

He looked at her skeptically "We will see."

She looked at him longingly but didn't push it any further. As she got to her feet she stumbled. He jumped to his feet and caught her. "Are you sure you're alright?"

"Yes, I'm fine. Just really tired. Now go, I need to get ready for school," she said, waving her hands at him.

"You're in my room."

She looked around, gave an embarrassed grin, and half danced to the bathroom. She closed his door, locked it and turned on the shower. She stripped and got in. Slowly she turned the hot water down until it was almost completely off. The cold water pelted off of her body as she leaned her head forward and against the shower wall masking the sound of her tears.

Lian got out of the shower and towelled herself off. She drew her name in the residue left on the mirror. She had stayed in the shower much longer than she had intended and knew that Bruce must be anxiously waiting to use it. She wrapped herself in a towel and unlocked his door. She wandered into her room and went straight for her desk. She opened her laptop to her lab assignment then poured herself a fresh cup of coffee. She tried to focus on her assignment but found her mind was wandering.

She looked in her closet at her meagre supply of clothes. She hadn't taken the time yet to replace much of what was destroyed after the break in. There was a small pile of potentially salvageable clothes on the bottom of her closet beside it and an even smaller pile of wearable clothes. The pile she tossed was bigger than the two of them combined. She grabbed a pair of jeans and tossed them on her bed and then threw a sweater to go with it. She grabbed her coffee and turned to face her bed.

Bruce was sitting on her bed under the clothes she had just thrown. She shrieked and jumped out of her skin, her towel slipping. She cursed him loudly as she clutched her towel, preventing it from falling any further.

"What the hell are you doing in here?"

"I'm sorry, I just couldn't wait any longer."

"I didn't finish my part of the assignment. I thought we could do it together in the lab." Lian blurted out.

"Don't be coy with me. You know what I'm talking about," he looked up at her; the longing in his eyes apparent.

"Bruce. I—" she stammered as he stood up and took her free hand.

"I'm not interested in those girls. I don't care about what they think or want. I don't care if they feel threatened by you.

They shouldn't, because there's no contest. You win hands down every time." She quietly sat down on her bed. He took both of her hands in his and kissed them gently. "I have never wanted anyone else. It has always been and always will be you." He leaned in and kissed her gently on the lips.

She felt her body involuntarily shiver and she fought against every single fibre of desire that burned inside her body, forcing herself not to return the kiss. But she couldn't stop herself from shedding a few tears before he finally broke off the kiss. He looked at her face and gently wiped the tears off. He took a deep breath and shook his head. "But its not me, is it?"

She slowly shook her head from side to side, biting her lower lip to hold back the tears. "I'm so sorry Bruce." She put her hand on his face and softly stroked his cheek. "I do love you. But like a brother," her heart wrenched at her words and she saw his eyes wash over with heartbreak. She lowered her hands into her lap, wringing them awkwardly. They stayed like this in silence and she could hear his heart shattering yet again. She had to hold her hands together to stop them from shaking.

Finally, he cleared his throat with a cough. "Well, it was worth a shot, wasn't it," Bruce said with fake cheerfulness. She looked at him apologetically, reaching a hand out towards him, but he turned on his heels and made his way back to his room. "See you later then," he said as he closed the door behind him.

As soon as the door clicked shut, tears exploded down her face. Her whole body trembled and she collapsed onto her bed. She grabbed her pillow and screamed into it. It was killing her to do this to him. She knew how much she was hurting him and how confused she was making him feel. But she was so confused and conflicted herself. She wished that she understood what was happening to her. She wished that she could tell him everything, so he'd understand. But how could she when she didn't even understand herself.

On the other side of her bathroom door Bruce stood still holding the door handle. He heard her start to cry before she was able to muffle the sound. Hesitantly, he walked through the bathroom, closed his door, leaned his back up against it and slid down it until he was sitting on the floor.

His face was full of tears and he shook his head from side to side muttering, "Why?" to himself as he cried.

Bruce was already seated when Lian walked into the classroom. It had been a week since his confession and aside from the classes they shared, he never saw her. She had been keeping her distance, as usual, albeit for different reasons now. She had spent more time away from the dorms than before and he could only speculate whom she was with. She came in holding a paper bag from their favourite cafe. She wouldn't even make eye contact with him as she made her way towards the back of the auditorium, her new seating of choice. He looked away as she passed his row and sighed. A moment later a blueberry muffin appeared on his desk. He turned to see one of his classmates rushing down the row away from him. He looked to the back and Lian was already seated with her notebook open and her eyes focused on the professor. He looked back to his muffin and shrugged his shoulders.

He pulled out his phone. He debated back and forth on whether or not he should send her a text. He wrote and erased several messages. Bruce was staring at the empty screen, when the professor cleared his throat to signal the start of class. He sighed and shoved his cell in his jacket pocket. As he did, he heard his phone vibrate. Exhaling softly, he looked at the professor, who was now pointing out anatomical references of an image on the big screen. He pulled his phone back out and read the text from Lian. *'I'm tired of the other girls being jealous of what's not there. Maybe this will make things easier for both of us.'* He looked at the message in surprise. Wiping the crumbs of the muffin off his lips, he tried to process what had just happened.

The professor rapped his ruler on his desk to gather everyone's attention. Bruce dropped his phone at the sound. It bounced off his lap, slid down his leg, and clattered onto the floor beneath. He quickly grabbed a pen and feigned taking notes as the class grew silent and the professor gave them all his best death stare. Everyone held their breath until the professor scoffed loudly but resumed with his lecture. Bruce relaxed a little and tried to focus on the lecture, but he was too perplexed by the mixed signals Lian was sending. He didn't understand what was going on.

A few kilometres off of campus was a dive bar called Chainsaw that was a regular for the students. Monday night was Bingo Night, Tuesday was Open Mic Night, Wednesday was Wing Wednesday, Thursday was Ladies Night, and the weekend was a mixture of western meets punk. It was the only bar Bruce had ever been in that could follow a crooning country ballad by daft punk without anyone batting an eye. It was a retrofitted log cabin with a pimped up interior; complete with a functioning fire pit in the centre of the bar and a variety of chainsaws adorning the wall. Rumour is that they were the same chainsaws used to cut down the logs to build the original cabin. He sat at the far end of the bar, away from the crowd, slowly sipping a pint.

"Drowning your sorrows are we?" the bartender asked, opening a bottle of Jack's and pouring Bruce a shot.

"I didn't ask for this."

The bartender nodded his head with a knowing look. "Didn't haft ta. It's on the house." He left the bottle next to

Bruce's pint and wandered down to the other end of the bar.

Bruce picked up the shot and looked it over carefully. Staring deeply and thoughtfully into it, he pondered his next move. He heard the bartender yell something unintelligible at him. Bruce raised the shot in the air in respect and then downed it. He followed it quickly with a swig of his beer and set the shot glass down.

A girl with long brown wavy hair that rippled well past her shoulders sat down beside him. She wore a cardigan sweater that was too tight and had a few too many buttons undone. She ran her hands over his shoulders and down his arms, cooing at his muscles. He chuckled, poured himself another shot, and downed it quickly. He held the empty shot glass in front of the girls face.

"This has more respect and intelligence then you do right now."

Her face flushed with anger as she squeaked in surprise, hopped off the barstool, and stormed off. The bartender came over, poured Bruce another shot, and poured one for himself. He tapped his shot glass against Bruces.

"I don't know if I should smack you for stupidity or shake your hand for brilliance. Well done lad. Down the hatch."

They both drank their shots and set their glasses down firmly. Bruce slipped a few bills his way but the bartender refused it. He smiled and walked away from Bruce, cleaning a glass as he did. Bruce slipped the bills over the counter and under a clean glass when his back was turned. As he leaned back down into his seat he turned to face the crowd. He could see a flock of girls crowding around a guy. He was chatting them up smoothly, comfortable with the attention. He stared enviously, wishing he could be that type of guy while also equally grateful that he wasn't. He had no one to blame but himself for the difficulty in his life. He changed career paths and flew halfway across the world with no one to blame but himself. He could have his choice of over a dozen girls - with several of them as intelligent and nice as they were beautiful - yet he had to want the one woman whom couldn't see him as anything more than a brother. He took another shot and finished his beer.

He turned his back to the crowd and played with his empty glass. The bartender tried to refill it but he refused and instead took the offer of a glass of water. A couple of girls approached him and sat on either side of him. One of them put a hand on his arm while the other asked how he was doing. He kept his focus straight ahead, at the bottles of alcohol behind the bar's counter, ignoring them, and hoping that they would take the hint and leave him be.

"Well, well, well. What have we here? Is someone brooding?" Darin said in a sing-song voice.

Bruce felt his hair on his neck stand on end as he turned to see Darin standing behind him. He slapped Bruces shoulder, gripped it, and squeezing it. "I wouldn't waste your time with this one ladies."

Bruce turned back to his water and the girls looked questioningly between Bruce and Darin.

Darin leaned in close, peering just over Bruce's shoulder. He was so close that Bruce could feel Darin's hot breath on his cheek. "Puppy's all house broken, isn't he? Even though his master prefers my chew toy over his."

Bruce jumped to his feet knocking over his barstool. The girls squealed and moved away quickly. Darin stumbled back laughing. Bruce charged him, grabbed Darin by his shirt, and pushed him backwards toward the nearest post. He slammed Darin - who was still laughing - into the post. Bruce let go of him and punched him in the face. Darin stumbled, grabbing his cheek, and looked up at Bruce. Darin's eyes glared and his lips curled up in a sneer. He stood upright and held his hand in front of him. He motioned towards himself, curling his fingers inwards, inviting Bruce to hit him again. Bruce swung and this time Darin stepped out of the way at the last second. Bruce's fist connected with the post instead. His body immediately buckled inwards while he clutched his fist. Darin kneed him in the stomach and caught him by the scruff of his hair as he fell over.

"Naughty puppy, shouldn't play with his master's toys," Darin said just before he punched Bruce squarely in the face.

Bruce fell to the ground. The room seeming to swirl around him as he fell. He could hear the bartender yelling at them to break up the fight and he could feel everyone around him scatter. A meek voice, soft and hesitant, asked if he was alright. He wasn't sure what he said in reply, but he thought the coolness of the cloth on his face was heaven. The angel in front of him cleaned his face and held an icepack to his cheek. The angel and the bartender helped him to his feet and sat him on a barstool. He took another shot graciously offered by the bartender and tried to get his eyes to focus clearly. The angel in front of him sorta looked like Lian, only her voice was softer. Her hair felt the same and her face felt just as soft. Even her lips felt the same. Although he couldn't be certain as he'd only kissed Lian once or twice. But they felt the same way they did in his dreams. They were soft, gentle, and delicate. She kissed him back eagerly and he responded hungrily.

He wasn't sure how long they had stayed in the bar making out, nor when or how they had left the bar and got into a cab. All he knew was that he had his hand up her shirt and her hand was down his pants and his mouth was on hers.

Chapter 12

Lian hid behind a building wishing she didn't have to be there to watch this debacle, but knowing there was no other way. Her hurt and betrayal was immense. It was even bigger than the sorrow that plagued her heart at what she was about to do.

A large crowd had filled the town centre where the temporary gallows had been erected. It was almost twenty feet in length and the largest they had yet and hopefully would ever have. The executioner was making his way across, checking that each noose was properly done. When he finished, he pulled the lever and twelve holes appeared beneath their respective nooses. He closed the floor up and then placed a small step stool beneath each noose. Once satisfied he gave a nod and made his way back to the far side where he waited.

A large group of mostly androgynous people, except for two - donned in simple white robes - slowly marched onto the gallows. They exchanged glances between each other with no words spoken. They appeared neither distressed nor upset - just calm and accepting. They each made their way behind a noose and stepped up onto the stool. The executioner began to dress each of their heads, one by one, with a bag and then tightened the noose around their necks. As Lian watched she felt her heart beating in her throat.

The time to act was nearing. When the executioner pulled that lever the group thought that they would simply disappear. That they would let their bodies jerk about momentarily and ruse death until the people were appeased. Then they would simply dissolve into thin air and leave behind the shell of a form. Little did they know that Lian had been suppressing their powers, day by day, since they were first arrested. Since this was the longest duration of time that the group had ever spent in their corporeal state amongst a single species, they had grown accustomed to trivial actions, such as eating and drinking. It hadn't taken much to convince the guards to give them some *last rites* wine. Lian recalled the initial remorse she felt when she had guilted them into staying on earth. Emotions were a complexity that they had little understanding of and as such they were easily manipulated. They had been unprepared for her emotional assault and due to their internal guilt from constantly pushing her away, they had been unable to resist her. They grew more and more accepting to their environment and, slowly but surely, more careless.

Lian turned away briefly, holding her hand close to her chest as she took a deep breath. Now was not the time to let herself be distracted by guilt. It was a luxury she couldn't afford. What they had done, or rather, what they were continuing to do was significantly worse than what she was about to do to them. She was only betraying a few people. It was a small handful compared to the entire universe they had betrayed. She would deceive this small group, even if within the group of the guilty were her own parents.

She wiped away her tears and turned to face the ever growing crowd. The executioner was more than halfway finished dressing them. Her parents stood at the end of the line. She took a deep breath and closed her eyes for a moment. In that moment, Auld and Eld, looked directly at her. They knew exactly what was happening and what she was about to do. But instead of anger filling their eyes there was sorrow and regret. Lian closed her eyes in anguish as they silenced their thoughts from her and the others. They had known for centuries that this moment was inevitable and could only hope that they had prepared her enough. Her parents mouthed silent apologies towards her.

As Lian opened her eyes her clothes dissipated into a black crop top, that slid partially off of her right shoulder, short black shorts, ankle high black boots, and a long black cape with hood that rippled in an invisible breeze. Upon closer examination you could see the constellations on the hood. In her right hand was a large scythe that stood two feet taller than herself. Tears streamed freely down her cheeks despite the grim and stony look on her face.

As the executioner dropped the hoods on her parents Lian raised her scythe high in the air, quietly muttering beneath her breath. She raised her other hand with it and a trail of smoke followed, ascending from the ground and whipping around her. It swept away from her cloak and away from her body as it slithered its way upwards until it reached the scythe. Lian's head was tilted up towards the sky as she chanted. She abruptly stopped chanting and snapped her head forward, looking directly at the gallows. The executioner pulled the handle as she slammed the scythe into the ground and cried out.

A ring of smoke flew out from the scythe and immediately engulfed those hanging. There was a brief flicker of light from the bodies but it was quickly snuffed out by the smoke. The crowd cheered as the bodies jerked about. They were unable to see the smoke, nor the brief flicker of light, nor how the smoke sucked the very souls out of their bodies and wrapped them all together into a neat bundle that came back to her. When the smoke returned to her, it deposited a palm sized piece of a ruby red stone into her hand. The stone glowed brightly before it burst into flames and flew directly into her chest. Lian looked at their lifeless bodies. They were unable to escape into their celestial forms as they had hoped. She gasped loudly as she realized that her parents, although hanging in their nooses, were holding hands. Her hand slid down the scythe as she crumbled to the ground. As she hit the earth the scythe turned into a dagger. Sobbing, she took the dagger with both of her hands, closed her eyes, and plunged it deep into her chest. But the dagger crumbled into dust as it touched her body. Lian wailed in agony and collapsed onto the ground, her whole body was wracked with sobs as she continued to cry. The dust in front of her swept up from the ground taking on the appearance of her parents. Lost in her sorrow and regret Lian didn't notice as they leaned down towards her.

Her parents kissed her on the forehead and whispered, "Forget."

Lian abruptly stopped crying. Her grim reaper clothes faded away and were replaced with a simple brown dress. Her eyes slowly closed as she rolled over onto her side and fell asleep. A light whirled around her and she became younger and younger until she barely a few days old. The dust outline of her parents dissipated until it was no more than a small speck of glittering black dust that flew into her eyelashes.

Screaming, Lian bolted upright in her bed, covered in a cold sweat, and chilled to the bone. Her blanket was on the floor and her bed sheets, damp with perspiration, lay askew on her legs. She was shaking violently as she looked out of her window and saw that it was still dark outside. A quick look at her clock showed that it was only three in the morning. She shivered as she wiped the sleep out of her eyes and then hugged herself, choking back the sobs. The moonlight cast shadows that danced on her walls, mocking her, urging her to fall asleep again so she could be tormented by her dreams once more.

She reached under the mattress and pulled out her dream journal. Absently, she flipped through the pages, a familiar routine that almost felt comforting, until she stopped at an entry dated almost fifteen years earlier. She would have been around seven years old when she wrote it. She scanned the entry, turned the page, and re-read it. Tears dropped onto the page, smearing the ink beneath them. She wiped them off of her face and dabbed the page with a tissue, careful not to damage the book.

At the end of the entry Lian had created a column with dates. The entry was about a nightmare she first had when she was barely five. For several years afterwards, whenever she would have the same nightmare, instead of rewriting it, she simply noted the date she had it. Even now the nightmare terrified her. But it also comforted her like an old blanket. She had been having the same nightmares for so long that they were starting to feel like an old friend. As she wrote todays date in the column something in the last sentence of the entry caught her eye. It was wrong. The nightmare she just had hadn't ended there. She flipped back a page and carefully re-read the entry. Word for word it was identical until the end. For the first time ever, the dream hadn't ended in the same place. She had always woken up after the executioner put the last bag over the final head in the line up.

She clawed at her chest as it suddenly grew hot. Hastily, she pulled her t-shirt off and looked down to discover an open wound on her chest. About the size of the blade from her dreams. Gingerly, she pressed her finger on it and winced as it hurt to touch. Clutching her chest her heart lurched heavily inside her. It thundered so loudly that she could feel her head rattle from side to side. She groaned, collapsing to her side, pulling her knees up and wrapping her arms around them. The intense pain in her chest continued to grow, threatening to engulf her entirely.

She pulled a hand away only to see it was covered in a red sticky substance that glittered with flecks of light in it. She looked down at her chest and saw small tendrils and slivers of a soft white light escaping from her wound. It burned her flesh as it made contact with her skin. The tendrils began to reach further down her body. Instinctively she clenched her hand around the tendrils, clawing at them, and trying to crush them in her hand. She would do anything to stop her chest from burning. Lian wailed as the pain in her chest increased and the tendrils danced about in her hand, twitching. She gritted her teeth through the pain and pulled herself to her feet. In only her underwear she stumbled her way across her room through the adjoining bathroom and into Bruce's room.

She called out to him in a whisper. The pain escalating greatly with each step that she took. She clutched the tendrils tightly in one hand and clutched her chest wound with the other. She called out to him again. Her voice was haggard and hoarse. She stumbled across the room towards his bed. Lian reached her one hand out to touch his back and rolled him towards her. Before she could call his name again she realized that *he* was actually a *she*. Bruce had a woman in his bed. Gasping softly she took a step backwards as the girl mumbled in her sleep and her eyelids flickered. Bruce's arm appeared out of nowhere and wrapped itself around the midsection of the mystery woman in his bed. Shocked and devastated Lian took another step backwards, before turning around completely and running back to her room.

Back in her bed Lian burst into anguished tears. As she cried herself to sleep, she barely took notice that her chest wound and the mysterious tendril had disappeared. The pain that she now felt was only in her heart.

Bruce leaned back in his chair, his legs stretched out. After last nights fiasco the girls had decided to give him space — aka avoid him. He was sure the rumours of his drunken misadventures, or lack there of, were already circulating in the cliques. He wasn't sure what he had been thinking. Truthfully, about a dozen beer and several shots in he was pretty sure there hadn't been any kind of thinking going on. While in some aspects it had felt good to let loose and be free, it only felt good the first couple of hours. He recalled being sullen and pushing everyone away. He had wanted to be alone in his misery, but the girls wouldn't give him space. He wasn't even sure whom he had woken up beside in the morning or how he had ended up with her. He could have sworn that he was an ass most of the night. The only thing that he really remembered was that he had tried to perform, but he couldn't. Guilt, angst, remorse, and beer had put a damper on his physical spirits.

He realized that he hadn't seen Auld and Eld in several days. So much for Lian being in dire need of rescuing. Bruce was again starting to believe that he had created them as an excuse to be her knight in shining armour. They justified his desires to be there for her. They justified him flying halfway across the world just to follow her.

The professor cleared his throat and then began his lecture. Bruce looked around, realizing that he hadn't seen Lian come in. He pulled out his phone and began composing a text to ask if she was alright, but stopped himself before he could send it. She didn't care about him so why should he care about her. He was just torturing himself. It was a vicious cycle that he needed to get himself out of. He deleted the text, shrugged his shoulders, hit record on his mini tape recorder, and began taking notes.

Chapter 13

A small village in Ireland

Fanai woke up to a cabin much darker than usual. It was so dark he thought that perhaps he had woken up in the middle of the night. He rubbed the sleep from his eyes and rolled over towards his nightstand. Turning the alarm clock towards him he realized that it was indeed morning and, in fact, well past his usual waking hour. He lay back down and reached all of his limbs outwards, like a starfish, groaning as he stretched his tired, old body out. He chuffed as he realized that he couldn't even remember how old he really was.

Pushing the blankets aside, he sat up and reluctantly set his feet on the floor; expecting to be rewarded with the usual morning chilliness. Much to his surprise the floor was only mildly cool. He smiled, thinking he had finally made a good choice in his penchant to overfill the fireplace with wood before sleep. He knew, by now, that where he lived seldom got cold, despite being buried deep in the mountains. However, he had an apparent love for a much warmer climate — a hint to his past, he supposed. Perhaps he was from Australia or somewhere else that was warm year round. The weather in this village was quite pleasant, but if it got anything lower than light sweater weather Fanai could feel the chill in his bones. He remembered the look on the cabin owner's face the first week the weather dipped down and he had requested enough wood to stock the entire village for the winter. Colin had thought he had gone mad. And perhaps, he was.

Fanai stumbled his way towards the kitchen and, in autopilot, assembled the makings of coffee. As he stood at the sink, cleaning his mug, he stared aimlessly out the window. It took a few moments before he was coherent enough to realize he couldn't actually see out the window and that it was covered completely in white. *Snow? Couldn't be,* he thought to himself. Colin swore that although they may see a small trickling of snow over the winter, it seldom got cold enough for much of it to stick to the ground. Frowning, he wandered over towards another window. It too was covered in snow, only slightly less so. He could make out the trickling of the sun beating down outside. He heard the coffee maker perk loudly and lost interest in the snow. He slipped on his slippers and poured himself a cup of coffee before sitting down at the kitchen island. He was more than halfway through his mug when he realized how cool it had become inside the cabin.

A quick glance at the fireplace revealed nothing but black soot. The last dying embers had been out for hours, yet the air was too warm for a night of no fire. Almost as if the cabin was insulated and had been long before the fire burnt out. Fanai jumped to his feet and ran to the front door, coffee still in hand. Without even a moments hesitation he pulled the door wide open. A mountain of soft, white, fluffy snow fell upon him, almost knocking him over in surprise; as opposed to sheer mass. Once he regained his senses he realized that there was almost two feet of snow standing outside. He closed the front door and shook whatever unmelted snow remained on him. Fallen snow swirled in his coffee mug. He laughed at his new found coffee whitener.

Water dripped down the sides of his face as the snow on his head melted. He sat back down surprised at the amount of snow that had fallen overnight. Setting his coffee down he turned on the radio. It was small, black and most likely from the sixties. It had come with the cabin and aside from his sketchbook was one of his most prized possessions. He had planned on asking Colin if he could keep it and buy a new one to replace it. He wasn't sure why he was attached to it, but like the girl, it drew him in. Perhaps, like him, the radio was just another old and forgotten relic of the past. It took a few minutes to find a local station that had news as he normally listened to a station that played non stop classical music. Fanai wasn't surprised when the first station he found wasn't playing music but instead the hosts were excitedly chattering non stop about the enormous amount of snow that had fallen overnight. That it was not only a record for their area, but for all of Ireland. As well, how neighbouring areas seemed to be unaffected by the snow and it was limited to this one tiny village only.

He listened as they explained different theories as to why the snow was falling and how long it would last. The skies seemed to have an endless supply of snow clouds. He was already on his second cup of coffee when he saw his sketchbook sitting open on the table. He walked over to it and saw her face.

Of course, how could he have forgotten her? Would she be outside? *Of course she would be,* he told himself. She always was. She was always waiting. She was waiting for something. She was waiting for someone. He wish he knew what or whom she was waiting for. He tried to shrug it off, that she wasn't his problem. If she chose to sit outside in this cold, freezing weather it was her choice. He flipped absently through the pages and could feel his longing for her growing. His heart ached more deeply then ever before. He knew, deep down inside, who she was waiting for. He had just been afraid to admit it out loud. Afraid to give up the one thing that had ruined not only his life, but everyone he had cared about.

His mug slipped through his fingers, shattering upon impact with the floor. Coffee splashed on his slippers and up the pant leg of his pyjamas. His wife, his child, his brother, and family were all dead. And it was all his fault. It was due to his greed and his selfishness. He had lied to himself, and to them. Calling it a passion. A right. But deep down inside he knew that he was simply afraid. And that he had dragged them all down with him. Destroyed the remainder of his people, the Nomdians, with his selfishness. Fanai suddenly knew why he was there and not just in this town or country, but why he was on this planet.

Without a moments hesitation he ran towards the door. He pulled on his rain boots, the closest thing he had to winter boots, and the heaviest sweater and jacket he could find. He threw his front door open again and ran out into the storm, ignoring the radio hosts urge that everyone remain inside.

The snow beat heavily upon him despite its lightness. Each flake felt like a slap to his face. His cheeks began to sting. They turned bright red, streaked by the tears that fell down his face. His hair quickly turned white and clumps of snow stuck to his head forming odd icicle like formations. His breath, hot and heavy by comparison of the air around him, came out of him in ragged breaths. His breath formed large white clouds, easily mistaken for the falling snow. He pumped his arms as fiercely as he could, pushing himself harder and harder against the molasses like snow. His heart raced frantically and his lungs burned. They screamed for air, but still he pushed on. Something inside him told him that time was scarce.

He rounded the first corner of fields and almost stopped in awe. The entire skyline was a blanket of white. The ground was white, the houses were white, and the air was pure white. He couldn't distinguish the ground in front of him from the post along the edge of the road or even from his own hands that he held out in front of him. The sky was dumping snow as far as the eye couldn't see and he suddenly grew afraid. Afraid that he wouldn't be able to find her, that he had waited too long to realize the truth and severity of the situation.

He stopped in the middle of the path. Although he couldn't see much, he just knew that he had found the stone fence. Carefully, trying to avoid falling into the ditch that lay between the road and the field, he stepped towards the edge of the road and through the ditch. His hands held out far in front of him. Feeling like a blind man in a dark room, he was fumbling, hoping, and wondering where the edge of the fence would be.

Finally he fell upon it and he cried out in happiness. He literally rolled himself over the fence, falling onto the ground beside it with a thud, causing the snow to fly upwards. He got back onto his feet, placed his hands on the top of the stone wall and felt his way along it. He looked far into the distance and was still unable to see anything beyond white. He couldn't even see the fence beneath his hands.

He walked for what seemed like hours - but couldn't be much more than a few minutes - when he finally saw her. The snow, much like the rain, fell everywhere but on her. Her dress swayed softly, like it always did and her hair fell, ever so, the same. Only this time, she was no longer looking out into the field, but directly at him. Her eyes, while still sad, had a trace of laughter in them. It was as if the sight of him in his pyjamas brought joy to her heart. He stopped at the edge of where the snow fell beside her and looked up at her with sorrow. His heart suddenly filled with shame, but she smiled at him fondly and tapped the space beside her. As she did, the snow retreated back towards him and left a space, large enough for another person, void of snowfall.

He stepped into her circle and sat down beside her. Then he quickly stood back up and shed his jacket and heavy sweater. He sat back down beside her. They both stared out at the fields together, silent with their thoughts.

Finally, he mustered the courage to speak to her. "I'm so sorry," was all he could force himself to say between choking sobs.

She put her hand on his and squeezed it tightly. "Would it comfort you to know that you are the first to say that to me?" she said softly.

He looked at her side profile, shocked. He couldn't believe that the others had been able to find peace with what they had done, after so much destruction had resulted in their actions. She turned to face him, her eyes full of sadness again.

"I wish you were the doctor," she said absently, not so much at him but just in general.

"I am a doctor, though. Did you want a specific one?" he asked her, curious.

She chuckled, "The doctor I want isn't even real. The doctor I want is but a dream of man. But a man who could relate to me. A man who understood how hard the passage of time is. Who understands how hard it is to do what is right, but does it regardless. A doctor, who may not be able to heal my heart, but would be able to sympathize with mine," she said softly and looked at him briefly, her eyes flickering. "But, he is nothing more than a dream. A figment of our imaginations."

The two of them looked out at the fields again, falling silent. She took his hand in hers and squeezed it firmly.

"Are you ready?" she asked him. He nodded and she smiled. "Lay your head down here and close your eyes," she said, instructing him to lay his head down on her lap. He did as he was told and gazed longingly into her eyes for a moment before closing his. She placed her left hand over his eyes and held the right hand up in the air. As she did a large skeletal scythe dyed crimson red appeared in her hand. Her dress quickly transformed from white into red and a black cape flowed from her shoulders.

Lian seemed to have skipped their next class together. When pressed, none of her classmates recalled seeing her in lab that morning either. She wasn't in her room when he had woken up, only his drunken companion. Bruce had locked the bathroom door on his side before he left so his sleeping beauty could rest uninterrupted. He pushed his way through the now seemingly overcrowded campus. He broke out in a panicked dash towards their dormitory, the crowd of students formed a seeming impenetrable wall. He ran up the staircase to the third floor and was sweating despite the still snowy and frosty spring weather outside. Bruce stormed into his own room, shouting out for Lian as soon as he had entered. He made his way through their shared bathroom and into her room.

Nothing was amiss in her room as far as he could tell. Her room was neat and tidy as usual and her bed made. He found her diary on her desk and flipped through it until he found the last entry. It talked about nothing more than her classes and her current lab work. He felt under her mattress for her dream journal. Flipping through it he was surprised at how full it had suddenly become. What intrigued him the most was Lian's most recent dream of a man in Ireland.

"A little bit of help would be great right now," Bruce shouted out loud as he sat down onto her bed. He slid the journal back under the mattress he put his hands onto his head and groaned. He was trying to figure out where she might have gone and why. Frustrated, he grabbed her pillow and threw it off the bed. He grabbed her blanket, then her sheets, and ripped them off in anger. When he had vented off enough steam, he looked at the bed dejected, and realized that he had made quite the mess. Bruce gathered her bedding and went about re-making it. As he did, her dream journal fell to the floor. He picked it up as he finished making Lian's bed and he went to put it back. Impulsively he opened it up again.

Moments ago he had been floored by how full it was. But upon closer examination, he was more surprised at the reoccurrence of some of her dreams. They had become a nightly event; sometimes more than one a night. The amount of detail they now had was also disturbing. After the first year of documenting her dreams they seldom strayed from the chain of events she first dreamt of. But in the past month alone they had become longer, more intense, and more detailed. But even more distressing, was the fact that she had recently started having them during the day and was waking in seemingly random places, far from where she could last recollect being.

He found an random entry, more meant for her diary then her dream journal.

"I'm coming to terms that the dreams are not merely dreams but memories of a past life. A life that was most likely mine and that wants to return. I'm scared of what I was and what I feel I have to do. I have a duty, it seems, and I think I'm trying to run away from it."

As he closed the book a polaroid picture slipped out and slid onto the floor. He picked it up and saw it was from their first hike after they had arrived. He knew where she was.

A galaxy not so far from the Milky Way

Auld lay on her back, her body covered in perspiration. Her hair was ragged and dishevelled but her eyes sparkling with joy. Eld stood above her, his face filled with awe and amazement. In his arms, he held a small bundle of blankets and inside it was a tiny creature — their creature. Her birth had been spectacular and awe inspiring. From the first time that Auld had revealed her new feminine features to the first time that they had made love, to now giving birth. Nothing could have prepared them for the onslaught of the unexpected the two of them would face. When the time had come, the rest of their people had fled in fear, leaving them to fend for themselves. Auld and Eld had been terrified and unsure of what to do or how to approach this foreign territory and were barely able to keep their thoughts away from the others.

They had been hiding on a planet for several months already and were midway through Auld's pregnancy when she found herself unable to shift out of her corporeal stage. So she and Eld had remained behind while the rest of their people idled about. The rest were utterly helpless without the two of them leading, yet too frightened to contribute in any helpful way. The group had tried, multiple times, to leave. They hadn't even made it out of the solar system when they were overcome with crippling uncertainty and anxiety, bringing them back to a nearby planet. After some time, the group moved themselves onto the same planet, slowly but surely nudging their way close enough to hear the neighbouring gossip of their leaders. The group was afraid to leave their leaders, and yet even more afraid to stay with them. The group was unable to assimilate the pregnancy of their leaders and feared the unknowingness of it.

When the time finally came, Auld found herself crippled by the pain inside and quickly took to the bed. Eld had spent much of his time on the planet researching birth from the villagers that lived nearby yet had been unable to gain much knowledge. The villagers were a quite primitive race and had yet to develop advanced medicine of any kind. Thankfully, Eld had found a hut on the far outreaches of the village; far from prying eyes. It was more than a days journey to the outskirts of the nearest village so it was unlikely that anyone would wander their way accidentally and see something that they shouldn't.

Eld prepared a basin of hot water and another of cold, with rags in both. Auld placed herself on her back with her legs bent and spread wide. Her dress hiked up to her waist as she did. He had lain a towel beneath her and they waited. Beyond that they had little to go on. The species on this planet gave birth through their stomach, with an opening appearing midsection when the child was ready to emerge. But, from what he had gathered, they also mated in a similar fashion. Eld had seen several couples wander the village, their stomachs begin to glow from beneath their clothing when they approached each other. With that understanding he made the deduction that the baby would emerge from where it was thusly put in. But, just to be safe, Auld wore loose clothing that was easily removable and together they had placed towels and rags under every square inch of her body.

Eld placed a cool cloth on her forehead as she assured him that she was alright. Auld then screamed out in agony as another contraction occurred. A moment later she was calm again while his heart lurched frantically inside his chest. She asked him if he could see anything so he lifted up her dress and looked at her stomach. Shaking his head he helped her roll to her side and looked up her dress. Again he shook his head and helped Auld lay down on her back where she felt most comfortable. Eld stood at her feet and looked between her legs, shaking his head. Auld screamed again and he jumped back as blue and white tendrils of light emerged from between her legs. They swirled in and out, forming a ball of light. More tendrils appeared; these ones were golden. They emerged outwards, attaching themselves to the ball. The shape pulsed rapidly as it took shape. A leg popped out from one end, an arm the other. A second leg pushed out and then a head popped out from the other end. The light flicked and faded, dissolving, until it left behind a perfectly formed baby girl.

Auld cried out, asking him what was wrong, but Eld found himself unable to form words with either his mouth or mind. The baby, their baby, was perfect. A mop of dark black hair with streaks of red throughout sat atop her head. Her skin was as white as snow. Her eyes were a bright vibrant green with flecks of blue in them. She looked just like her mother. Eld marvelled at this. Not only at the fact that he and Auld had developed gender for the first time when they had mated, but that they had retained said genders. Now their child was born with one. He wondered if she would change gender as she grew, but his heart told him otherwise.

Eld picked their daughter up, wrapping her in a towel and holding her close to his chest as she cooed. Smiling, he turned to Auld and held the baby out towards her. Auld reached out with eager arms and scooped the baby from him quickly. He sat down next to them and smiled. It was, unfortunately, short lived. Auld looked up, her face grim.

"She's perfect isn't she?" Auld asked softly and Eld nodded in agreement. "But we only have her for a short time, don't we?" she asked rhetorically, her eyes tearing up.

"We must make the most of this miracle that has been

bestowed upon us. We mustn't be sad, we should rejoice," Eld replied and Auld nodded in agreement. But her heart grew heavy and a lump formed in her throat. He stroked her hair softly and kissed her on the forehead.

"We can not let the others know what we know. Ever. They wouldn't understand and they'd make us kill her while we still could," Auld said, her hands trembling. This innocent child, this babe of hers, looked up at her with unsuspecting eyes. They would protect her at all costs; from her family, her people, and anyone else that would seek her out. They would raise her as their own, teach her the ways of their people, and teach her how to harness her powers. But they would also teach her how to keep secrets. Teach her which ones she must keep at all costs. Help her wield her true powers. They would raise her to be strong and independent.

"Yes, but we also must keep it a secret it from her as well."

Auld looked at him with confusion, "But how can we help her if she doesn't know who she is?"

Eld looked down at his daughter and smiled fondly. "In time, she will know who she is and what she is to do. We needn't tell her that. I imagine it has been ingrained into her very core. If she knew that we knew the truth it would make what she has to eventually do all the more difficult. As her parents we will raise her to be strong, to hide secrets from us and the others, but we will never, ever, let her know our truth. We can not."

"But—" Auld started to say, but let her words falter. He was right. It was the sacrifice they had to make for their child. She couldn't even begin to imagine how difficult it would be for their daughter when she realized that her responsibilities would include killing her own family. If she found out that her parents raised her knowing this, it would be too much for her to bear.

"Each and every day from now, until the very end, we

must prepare. Not only do we have to raise her, but we have to prepare for the eventual heart break; to protect her until our very last moment. We need to give her the strength she needs to succeed. At all costs." Eld said grimly, yet his voice was filled with pride.

They both looked down at their baby. Their love and joy was mixed with heartbreak and sorrow. They looked at each other, their eyes grim, but determined, and nodded in agreement.

"We will love her immensely," Auld said softly.

Chapter 14

The sky was blossoming brilliant red and pink hues as the sun began to set. Bruce was severely underdressed for this time of night but he knew that time was of the essence. Auld and Eld had appeared at the base of the mountain, assuring him that Lian's presence was nearby. But that it was also very weak. They were quite confused as to why her presence was fluctuating. As the sun began its final descent into the ground Bruce reached into his pocket and, being the boy scout that he was, pulled out a glow stick. He snapped and shook it quickly. Then held it just above his head. The light it provided was mediocre but his flashlight was on the verge of dying and he wanted to preserve it in very likely event of an emergency.

His heart was racing as he trekked his way up the mountain trail as fast as humanly possible. Something was very, very wrong. Every fibre of his being told him that Lian was in trouble — that they were all in trouble. He felt a shift in the wind. As the air thickened, it stifled his breath. Bruce knew that if he didn't get to Lian soon he would lose her forever. A breeze picked up and whipped a tree branch into his face as Auld and Eld materialized in front of him. They were more ghost like in appearance and their voices were breaking up like a bad phone connection. They were in the beginnings of a feverish panic, but he managed to ascertain that they had found Lian further up ahead. Bruce burst into a frenzied run as he crested the top of the mountain. As soon as he made his way into the clearing Auld and Eld disappeared only to rematerialized a few feet in front of him. Lightening crashed silently against the cloudless sky illuminating the whole mountaintop. Bruce saw Lian lying unconscious on the ground.

Dropping down to his knees beside her, Bruce set the glow stick on the ground and reached to grab her when she flickered briefly - like a disrupted channel on a television set from the eighties with rabbit ears - before disappearing. He touched the ground where she had just been and looked up at Auld in surprise. They were holding each other tight with the same look of anxiousness and surprise on their faces.

"Where did she go?" Bruce asked bewildered. "What just happened?"

Eld looked at him baffled and Bruce shook his head in disbelief. As he touched the ground he felt it rapidly growing hotter by the second. He pulled his hand away quickly as the empty space above the ground flickered and wavered just before Lian reappeared. She was lying on her side, curled up into a ball and crying. She screamed out in pain as Bruce grabbed her shoulder and called out to her. Lian looked up at him; confused and disorientated. As he pulled her to a seated position Lian tried to push herself away. Bruce grabbed her arm but she struggled to free herself as she again flickered before disappearing. The wind snapped around him. The sky grumbled loudly as lightening crackled through the still clear and cloudless night. The mountain began to shake violently beneath them.

"Jesus Christ! What the hell is happening?" Bruce cried out

as the space above him distorted and Lian re-appeared directly onto his lap. He immediately wrapped his arms around her and she smiled at him weakly.

"Always doing foolish things aren't we?" Lian said as she began to fade away again.

Bruce gripped her more tightly, "Don't you leave me," he ordered and instead they both disappeared.

Bruce felt relief wash over him and tightened his grip on her hand with both of his.   "I have no idea. You disappeared from the group and then there were these wolves and—" his voice trailed off as he realized that he and Lian were no longer on the mountain top, but that he was in a dream that he had on the plane several months ago. That they were surrounded not only by the wolves, but several other animals. They were all gathered in the small opening around the pond in a forest.

They looked around slowly, frozen in place, unable to do much more than crane their heads from side to side. Bears, deer, moose, birds, rabbits, every animal you could think of - regardless of whether or not they should be in hibernation or have already migrated elsewhere - surrounded them. The animals filled every nook and cranny of space available in the small clearing around the pond. The pond itself, aside from the lead wolf, was empty. The animals skirted the edges of the pond. He could feel all of their eyes gazing upon them — upon her.

"I think we should leave now," Bruce said. His voice a mere whisper.

Lian shook her head and stood up.   "I don't think they'll let me leave," She replied softly and took a step further away from him. Their fingers lingered at the tips.

Bruce followed Lian's gaze and saw that the wolves were standing between the two of them. He took a small step towards her and they uttered a low, guttural growl. It was a warning. Lian could not leave the pond nor could Bruce get any closer.

Bruce shook his head in disbelief. "Don't," he urged her, unsure of what he was asking her not to do. He wasn't scared, but he certainly wasn't comfortable by any means. Something odd was about to happen and he wasn't sure if he wanted to be witness to it or not. Or if he even had a choice anymore.

Bruce leaned forward and took Lian's hand, tightening his grip briefly. She squeezed back and smiled bleakly. Tears softly sliding down her cheek as she mouthed the words, *"It'll be okay,"*. Her eyes once again filled with the milky blue light. Shaking his head from side to side, unwilling to give into whatever was happening, Bruce tried to pulled Lian towards him one last time. She gave him a firm squeeze that almost broke his fingers. Bruce gasped as Lian turned his hand over, kissed his palm, and held it to her cheek. She closed her eyes and sighed heavily. Then she let go of his hand and turned her back to him.

When they re-appeared the mountain had stopped trembling and Lian was still sitting in Bruce's lap. He pulled her closer, clutching her tightly. Lightening crackled across the sky with brilliant colours directly above them. Auld and Eld huddled together as the wind began to whip anything and everything that wasn't tied down off of the ground.

"What the hell is happening?" Bruce yelled out at Eld.

Lian shivered. "I don't —" she started to say but stopped when she realized Bruce wasn't talking to her. She followed his gaze but couldn't see anyone. "Bruce?"

Bruce gave Auld a stern look. Lian called out to Bruce again and he looked down at her tenderly.

"Don't ever leave me." He said to Lian firmly.

"I'm dying Bruce. My whole body feels like its being torn apart from the inside out," she sobbed, clinging to him as her body started to fade away again.

This time the mountain shook and trembled so violently that a portion of the nearby cliff crumbled off, thundering its way down. Bright, white lightening bore down and forced its way through a nearby tree. Lian shrieked and pushed herself away from Bruce; his grip having loosened slightly. She disappeared and for a brief moment everything around him went quiet. Bruce scrambled to his feet and shouted out for her. He ran over to Auld and Eld, trying to grab Eld's shoulders, forgetting that they were transparent and fell through them, landing face first onto the ground behind them.

"Where the hell is she?" Bruce roared at them.

They looked at each other, nodded silently, and looked back at Bruce. "The universe is reacting to her indecision," Eld said. "She needs to make a choice."

"A choice?" Bruce echoed.

"To live or die." Auld said solemnly.

"Is that a trick question?"

They looked at each other again as the air grew distorted and Lian faded back into existence. Her clothes were soaked and her skin glowed as it began to take on a translucent look.

"She can no longer exist as she has been. The universe cannot handle it anymore. She must choose to be whom she really is inside. Or she and everything will cease to exist."

"Why is that so hard for her to do?" Bruce asked frantically, glancing over at Lian shivering on the ground before she disappeared again and everything grew quiet.

"Only she can answer that question." Auld whispered.

"So what the hell can I do?" Bruce roared.

Lian reappeared in front of Bruce and he grabbed her, pulling her onto his arms. She was weak and freezing cold to the touch. He held her tight, crying into her hair. "Please Lian, please stay. Don't leave me."

Her eyes flickered as lighting crackled across the sky. "Let me go Bruce."

"Never."

"You don't know who I am."

"Of course I do. I've known you my whole life."

"Not who I really am."

"Who you are now is whatever you want to be and whom you've always been. That will never change. No matter what you become, you'll always be my Lian." Bruce insisted.

Lian smiled weakly. "I've done terrible things."

"I don't believe you. You'd never do anything without a good reason. Even if it was something horrible." Bruce grabbed her hand and squeezed it tightly. The mountain shook violently and her skin began to glow.

Lian cried out in pain as the stars above began to pulse erratically in the sky and then abruptly they popped out of existence. Like someone was systematically switching them off. Lian looked up at Bruce, her eyes full of tears that sparkled like diamonds. "You have to let me go," she pleaded.

Bruce shook his head, *"no"*. She curled up, her body clenched; fighting against the pain. The wind grew violent and began to whip at them relentlessly. Bruce pulled Lian closer. The sky was half dark, as the stars continued to disappear. Her parents slowly stepped towards them. Lian began to convulse as her skin grew more translucent. Lightening burst out of the sky and struck them both. Auld screamed in horror as the two of them disappeared in a flash.

Lian looked up into the sky. The bright moonlight penetrated the trees and basked in her nakedness. Looking down at the pond she continued forward. The lead wolf stepped aside, bowing slightly as she continued on. The water quickly ascended her body. It climbed up to her knees, her waist, her breast, and finally her neck. Without any hesitation Lian continued onwards until she was fully submerged into the water. Bruce screamed out her name as she disappeared. He fell to his knees crying. The wolves sat down, facing Bruce, and whimpered softly. He clenched his hands into tight fists and pounded the ground. One of the wolves licked the side of Bruce's face, as if consoling him. Instinctively he rubbed the side of the wolf's head, scratching his ears. The wolf nuzzled his head beneath Bruce's hand and pushed Bruce up to a sitting position. He looked at the wolf with his face full of anger. He was about to reprimand the wolf for getting in his way, when he realized that the wolves were no longer paying him any attention.

Instead, they were focused on the pond which had gone from a dark inky, blue-black, to the same milky blue colour he had seen in Lian's eyes. Bruce got to his feet and tried to stumble towards the pond, but the wolves yet again stopped him. However, it appeared that they were shaking their heads from side to side. To warn him of the danger if he entered the pond.

The ground beneath him began to rumble softly and the trees began to sway in an imaginary wind Bruce couldn't quite feel. The animals closest to the pond squawked and squealed, quickly moving away from the waters edge. The moonlight grew brighter by the second and its reflection on the pond grew larger just as quickly. It was as if the moon was somehow getting closer to the earth. The water began to ripple. It started from the spot he had seen her last and worked its way outwards. A low grumbling noise could be heard from all around. The trees groaned as they swayed and the bushes rustled nosily. The water began to surge violently and a breeze appeared blowing in a contrasting direction to the movement of the trees. Bruce fought to hold himself in one spot. The wolves refused to leave their post in front of him but they whimpered and mewled loudly; backing themselves up against him as they moved as far away from the waters edge as possible. The milky blue light began to pulse. It happened slowly at first and increased rapidly.

Then, just as everything grew to a crescendo and Bruce was convinced the world was about to end in that very spot alone, everything grew abruptly still. The water stopped moving entirely. The ripples dissipated, the wind stopped, the trees ceased their swaying, the moonlight was barely visible, and the light from inside the pond was gone.

Cautiously, Bruce took a step forward, cocking his head sideways and looked into the pond. A bright beam of blue light, three feet in diameter, appeared in the sky above and blasted straight into the pond. Where it hit, the water immediately parted. The circular beam of light continued to spread and grow quickly, forcing the water outwards, where it solidified into ice. The ice glittered and sparkled in the moonlight like escaping waves trying to reach the shore.

The momentum of the water gushing to the sides blew fiercely at Bruce. The water pushed him and the wolves backwards as they tried to stand their ground, only to end up sliding on their feet as the burst of air was too much. The wind, like an explosion, blasted Bruce off of his feet and sent him flying him backwards. A large brown bear broke his flight, mid air, and literally embraced him in a bear hug before lowering him safely down to the ground. Bruce pulled himself to his feet and turned to look back at the now empty pond.

The entire pond was void of water and what remained resembled that of a meteorite crash site. Where Lian once stood was the point of impact. Bruce screamed out her name and rushed towards the ponds edge, his feet stumbling over each other. He tripped over one of the wolves and fell flat onto his face. Choking back the sobs Bruce pulled himself to his knees as blood dripped down his left cheek. The ground around the ponds edge was now sharp with the blasted waters ice crystals. Bruce cried out Lian's name as he leaned back and stared up into the sky.

A soft gush of wind blew by his face and it carried with him the sound of Lian's voice. Bruce looked down and saw that in the centre of the pond, where Lian had just disappeared from, was a very large figure. It stood nearly twenty feet tall, its shape resembling that of a human. Instead of flesh its body was composed of a milky blue light. It was the same light that he had just seen in her eyes.

Very slowly, Bruce stood up and took her in. Lian was beautiful. Her skin was smooth and not smooth at the same time. It rippled and fluctuated with waves of light and colour, flowing from opaque to transparent seamlessly. Lian's hair, or what could be interpreted as hair, flowed down well past her shoulders and down to her knees. Her head tilted upwards as she looked up into the sky.

As Bruce took a step towards Lian, he felt the ground shake beneath him. The wolves yelped and jumped back, away from her. Bruce looked around and could see the other animals were frightened as well. He took a deep breath and continued to make his way towards her. The ground, already slippery with the ice, began to tremble and rumble beneath each step he took. At first, Bruce thought that earth was still going to end and that the danger had yet to pass. But then he realized that Lian's body was trembling and the ground was shaking in sync with her.

Bruce stopped when he was within arms reach and without even a forethought he reached out and touched her leg as he called out her name. As he made contact with Lian's skin he felt his mind explode from the inside out. Within a split second Bruce knew he had to make a choice — stay or leave. He needed to suffer the consequences of staying with her or suffer the consequences of abandoning her. Bruce didn't understand the repercussions of either of his choices; only that death was most likely imminent in both. But he didn't care what happened to him. Only what happened to Lian. In the moment that he had touched Lian he had felt her pain. Lian was hurting in ways he might never understand. But she was hurting and if he abandoned her now the hurt would amplify in ways she could not nor should not have to handle.

Bruce increased his grip on her, feeling her resist. His desire to stay with her was strong even as she fought to force him away. His head was splitting from the inside out. Bruce wasn't sure if it was going to implode, explode, or just simply cease to exist. Like a computer absorbing new data, images flashed through his head at an alarming rate. It was faster than his mind could process. The images encompassed lifetime after lifetime of her existence in a human shell. Lian wasn't human. She was an alien; a very old alien. Bruce saw her births, her deaths, her actions, and her responsibilities that weighed heavily on her heart. She took life, gave life, and lost her own. She lost herself again and again. Bruce saw the tears that never ceased flowing. He saw her as a human; lost without her memories and powerless. He saw her take back what she had to take and then die in an instant as she absorbed the power. It consumed her mind, body and soul. The realization of who she was flashed briefly in her eyes. Bruce saw Lian scream out in horror at the pain and then at the immense sadness that immediately followed.

But he didn't let go. Bruce wrapped his arms around Lian's leg and called out to her with his thoughts. He knew Lian would never hear his voice otherwise. Bruce told Lian that he loved her and begged for her to reach inside of him and to find the happiness that she gave him. He begged her to feel the love and joy she had brought to not only him, but to their friends. He promised to never let her go; no matter how bad things might get. Bruce promised that he would always be with her.

A warm wind enveloped him from the ground. Bruce opened his eyes and saw Lian's body flicker. In an instant she shrank down until she was the same size that she had always been. His arms were now embracing Lian from the back and were wrapped snuggly around her chest. Lian's head was tilted down into his arms. Bruce let go of Lian and turned her around to face him. Her eyes glittered green against her blue, transparent energy form. Bruce grabbed Lian by the sides of her face, drew her in, and kissed her. As he did ripples of a blueish white light emanated from her body as she began to take on a more solid form.

They broke apart their from kiss and Lian looked up into his eyes. Bruce could feel himself falling deeper and deeper into them. He could see the hesitation in her eyes, the desperation, and the loneliness. Bruce smiled softly and kissed Lian again with even more passion. As he pulled her in close, the light of her body flashed outwards and dissipated into the night air. What remained, was her human body once again. Bruce scooped her up into his arms and with their animal escorts, disappeared into the forest.

Bruce stepped clear of the forest and they reappeared on the mountain top. Still holding Lian he collapsed to his knees, momentarily losing consciousness.

"Bruce? Bruce?" Lian cried out. "Bruce. Wake up."

Bruce moaned softly and his eyes flickered open. A sly smile curled onto his lips. "Can't get rid of me that easily."

Lian's laughter quickly turned into sobs as she slid out of his arms and onto the ground. "Please Bruce, I don't deserve to live. Look around you. Look at what's happening. All because of me."

Bruce stood up and pulled Lian to her feet. He grabbed her by the shoulders and looked her straight in the eyes. "So make it stop," he said, a new founded sense of purpose in his voice. "Choose to live. Right here. Right now. For me. For us."

Lian looked at Bruce confused, as he slid a hand along the side of her face, drew her in close, and kissed her again. His kiss was soft at first then grew hungrily. Steam poured off of her skin as it became a translucent milky white that glittered softly. They broke apart their kiss; their lips still lingering softly on each other. Lian opened her eyes and looked up at the darkening sky.

Bruce pulled her chin down to face him and stared deeply into her eyes, "I love you."

Lian nodded back slowly and tears filled her eyes. "I love you too." She whispered as he kissed her again. Her shirt split in the back and several tendrils, comprised entirely of light, burst out of her back. The tendrils intricately weaved themselves into two large wings.

She opened her eyes to see a giant grin of wonder on his face. She glanced over her shoulder to try and see what he was looking at, but could only catch small glimpses of light behind her. She looked at her arms on his shoulder and gasped with surprise as she realized most of her body was covered in patches of translucent light. Lian looked up at Bruce's smiling face. Her jaw dropped suddenly as she saw Auld and Eld behind him.

Bruce turned to look at them and then back at Lian. "You can see them now?" he asked incredulously. "Do you know who they are?"

Lian nodded as crystal tears filled her eyes. Her parents stepped forward and knelt down before them. They looked at Bruce first.

"Protect her with your heart. Her future is entwined with yours as much as yours is entwined with hers." they said in unison.

Bruce barely noticed that their words were heard inside his mind and that their lips were no longer moving. He nodded as they turned to face Lian. Her eyes were glistening over with tears.

"Mother. Father." The pain of all their betrayals apparent on Lian's face. "I'm so sorry—" she started but her mother cut her off with a shake of her head.

Auld reached up gently stroked Lian's face. "Hush, my little one. You need to be brave now. You've a lot to do still, but you're almost done."

Lian gasped softly. "You knew?"

"We are so proud of you." Eld said as he smiled. "More than you'll ever know."

Auld and Eld began to slowly dissipate, back into the dust they once were. Lian pulled against Bruce's arms and he let her go as she reached out towards her parents.

"Don't go. I have so much I —" she started to say but was cut off but her own piercing shriek. She flung backwards, arching her back. Bruce barely had time to catch her as a beam of bright white light shot out from her chest and into the sky. He could barely hold her in place as the light poured out, breaking off into tendrils of brilliant white, blues, and pink that wrapped around the two of them. Her parents further dissipated and the last thing Lian heard was her parents telling her that they forgave her before another spasm hit her body and her parents disappeared completely.

Bruce held Lian close as she fought the urge to pull herself upright. When the spasm passed Lian wrapped her arms around Bruce's neck. They placed their heads on each others shoulders as the light continued to wrap around until it had fully consumed them both. It pulsed like a rapid heartbeat and pierced the night sky like a beacon from a lighthouse as Lian finally felt herself awaken.

To be continued....